12/05

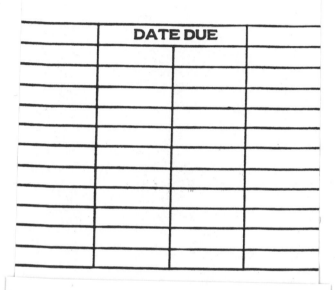

DATE DUE

KISSING
BRENDAN
CALLAHAN

KISSING BRENDAN CALLAHAN

SUSAN AMESSÉ

A Deborah Brodie Book
ROARING BROOK PRESS
New Milford, Connecticut

A DEBORAH BRODIE BOOK
Published by Roaring Brook Press
Roaring Brook Press is a division of Holtzbrinck Publishing
Holdings Limited Partnership
143 West Street, New Milford, Connecticut 06776

LIBRARY OF CONGRESS CATALOGING-IN-PUBLICATION DATA
Amessé, Susan.
    Kissing Brendan Callahan / Susan Amessé.—1st ed.
            p. cm.
    "A Deborah Brodie book."
    Summary: Sarah Simmons dreams of becoming a writer like her idol,
romance novelist Antonia DeMarco, but when Mom stops her from entering
a writing contest, the twelve-year-old resorts to subterfuge.
    ISBN 1-59643-015-X
[1. Authors—Fiction. 2. Mothers and daughters—Fiction. 3. Contests—Fiction.
4. Honesty—Fiction.] I. Title.
    PZ7.A5156Ki 2005
    [Fic]—dc22

10 9 8 7 6 5 4 3 2 1

Roaring Brook Press books are available for special promotions and premiums.
For details, contact: Director of Special Markets, Holtzbrinck Publishers.

BOOK DESIGN BY BTDNYC
Printed in the United States of America
First edition October 2005

To my husband, Tom

For all the love, support, inspiration, and laughter

ACKNOWLEDGMENTS

Heartfelt thanks to my editor, Deborah Brodie. You've always inspired me to chisel deeper and find what lies beneath the marble. It has been a privilege to work with you.

I am especially grateful to Michelle de Savigny for her encouragement and her readiness to read draft after draft with unflinching energy and thoughtfulness.

A multitude of thank-yous to the folks who were kind enough to read various drafts of this book and offer suggestions. Your generosity and camaraderie have warmed my soul. They include: Roberta Davidson Bender, Barbara Baker, Susan Marston, Jessica Feder-Birnbaum, Betsey Day, Susan Grillo, Grace Sells, Kathy Mignano, Maureen Marlow and Loretta Holz.

Hugs and kisses to my family and friends who always bothered to ask, How's the writing going?

And my undying gratitude to my husband, Tom, for his boundless support in encouraging me to pursue my dream of becoming a children's book writer and never, ever letting me give up. Thanks for reading and critiquing every draft of this book. I couldn't have finished it without you.

KISSING
BRENDAN
CALLAHAN

"*Do you have what it takes to be a royal princess? Take the test and find out.*"

Our checkout line isn't moving, so I grab a copy of *Teen Romance* from the rack next to the register. On the cover is a smiling Princess Agnes of Hortonia. I flip through the magazine until I find the story about her and the princess quiz. If only I could be whisked away from Granneli's Supermarket to a castle with turrets and a moat. Besides, I love purple, which everyone knows is a royal color.

Question one: *A princess must be prepared to make many public appearances. Are you shy around strangers?*

A: Always. B: Sometimes. C: Absolutely not.

My answer is B, but I wish it were C.

Question two: *A princess often travels to foreign countries to speak about important issues. How many languages can you speak?*

A: Two. B: Three. C: Four or more.

Let's see. Besides English, I know a few French words because it's such a romantic language. And I can say thank you in Portuguese. I pick B as my answer.

"Bonjour!" I give my brother, Jason, my finest princess wave, but he continues to sleep comfortably in his baby carrier among our groceries.

"Did you get a good shot of the accident?" my mother says into her cell phone. "It's for the front page." I, Princess Sarah, wave at Mom, but she's not looking.

I take out my notebook, which I carry with me at all times, and jot down a few notes about being a princess. I'm planning to be a best-selling author of high-quality romances.

On to **Question three**: *A princess must always exhibit poise and courtesy. If you were attending an official reception and noticed someone's wig falling off, how would you react?*

A: Laugh and point. B: Ask them to leave immediately. C: Divert attention to give the unfortunate person time to fix her wig.

Absolutely, answer C. I turn toward a five-foot-tall stack of canned beans, today's Super Smart Buy. *"Enchanté!* Oh, look over there," I say regally. "The queen has arrived."

"Where?"

I turn. It's Brendan Callahan. He smirks. "Talking to yourself again?"

"I'm talking to my baby brother," I say.

"Right." He plucks the magazine out of my hand. He bats his eyelashes and puts on a high, silly voice. "Do you have what it takes to be a royal princess?" He looks at me and laughs. "No way could you be a princess."

I grab the magazine. "And why not?"

"Look at the first question. You're not good with strangers."

"I am too."

"You're totally shy," he says. "You could take a lesson from me. I have a wonderful, outgoing personality. And I know how to dress with style." He poses so I can see the dumb T-shirt he's wearing. This one says, "I don't suffer from insanity, I enjoy every minute of it."

I eye Jason, hoping he'll wake up and cry or something.

"Hey," says Brendan. "How do you get a baby astronaut to sleep? You rock-it. Get it?"

"Got it."

Wake up, Jason!

"You'll love this one," he says. "A woman calls her doctor. 'Doctor, doctor,' she says, 'my baby's swallowed a bullet.' The doctor says, 'Well, don't point him at anyone until I get there.'"

Ha. Ha. Ha.

"Brendan." My mother waves and pulls the cell phone away from her ear. "It's good to see you. Why don't you drop by later? It's been ages since you and Sarah played chess."

"I'm busy," he says.

"Me too."

Mom raises an eyebrow at me. "Perhaps another

time, Brendan. Tell your mother we need to talk about the Preservation Fair. Is she here?"

Brendan shrugs. "She's somewhere."

Mom nods and resumes her phone conversation—something about a factory strike.

Brendan looks over his shoulder. "I have to get out of here. The guys are getting a basketball game together at P.S. 43 and they need me."

"So?" I say.

"I ditched my mother in the produce aisle. If you happen to bump into her, forget you've seen me."

"That won't be hard," I say.

He leans in. "You should check out aisle five. Good humor is on sale." He backs away, pretending to dribble a ball.

In my notebook, I write *Brendan Callahan—jerk,* and underline it. Then I write a reminder to e-mail Lynn as soon as I get home. Before she left to visit her father in San Francisco, she sat on my bed listing the cutest boys at Hamilton Intermediate School and Brendan was on the list. It is my duty as her best friend to point out his flaws, as there are so many of them.

"Martha, listen to me," says my mother. "We cannot do a feature about a psychic. We get little respect being a Staten Island newspaper as it is."

"Mom," I say. "I'd love to read about a psychic." She shushes me.

"When I stop by the office, we'll talk." She clicks off the phone and we begin piling groceries on the belt.

"Mom, no one has ever written about a day in the life of a psychic."

"And with good reason," she says. "Pass the grapes."

"You're being closed-minded."

"Sweetie, our readers count on us for accuracy."

"Accuracy isn't everything," I insist.

"Yes, it is."

The cashier rings up our groceries and I help bag them. On the way out, I see a circus poster.

"Mom," I say, pointing. "Can we go? There's a show this afternoon."

"It sounds like fun," she says. "But I have to stop by the office."

"You're on maternity leave. Doesn't that mean that you don't go to the office every day? Isn't this the time to bond with your children?"

She wheels the cart across the steamy parking lot. "I only drop in for a few minutes. You wouldn't want the *Courier* to fall apart without me."

"What if *I* should fall apart without *you*?"

"What, honey?"

"Nothing." She straps Jason's baby seat in while I put the groceries in the trunk of our Volvo.

On the way to the office, I take out my notebook

and begin a new story. It's about a lonely but talented contortionist named Roxanne. A circus comes to town, and the owner sees Roxanne performing in a supermarket for her baby brother, bending herself into a pretzel. "What a talent!" he says. "You must join my circus."

"Please, mother," begs Roxanne. Her mother refuses because she has been put under a spell by an evil spirit lurking in her cell phone.

When we get to Mom's office, she runs ahead. As I carry Jason into the building, I imagine myself an ace reporter like my mother used to be. I'd race to the scene of the crime, interview the witnesses, and solve the mystery all by myself. I wish I could lead such an exciting writer's life.

The newsroom is full of activity. Along the sides are offices, but most of the floor is just a large, open area crammed with desks. Many of the reporters and editors are typing stories into their computers or talking on the phone. It's so loud that I wonder how any of them can concentrate.

Mom is in her office talking with the assistant editor, Joe. They're arguing about something and Mom pulls at her hair. She's been doing this a lot lately and it worries me. Before the baby, her short brown hair was always neatly styled, but the constant pulling is creating tiny spikes on the top of her head. She almost looks like a punk rocker instead of a managing editor. I carry Jason back into the newsroom.

"Hey, cutie," says a deep voice. I turn around. It's Filipe Santo, the sportswriter. He walks toward me and I lean in to kiss Jason because I don't want Filipe to see that I'm blushing. Filipe is so handsome! So tanned! So exotic! It's because of him I know how to say thank you in Portuguese. *Obrigado.*

"You're going to be a hit with the ladies," he tells Jason, pinching his cheek. I was hoping he thought I was cute.

"How's it going, Sarah?"

"Uh." I stare at his lips, wondering if his slim moustache would tickle if he kissed me.

"Well," he says. "Got to run."

"Right," I say to his back. "Obrigado!" He leaves behind a mist of musk aftershave.

"Oo goo goo goo. Can I hold the kid?" I hand Jason over to Cynthia, the restaurant critic. "Oo goo goo goo," she says. "What a gootie, gootie cutie. Oo goo goo goo."

"Hey, Sarah." Anne Marie Valgetti leans back in her chair and waves me over. "What's doing?"

"Nothing much," I answer. Anne Marie and I are both going to be in the seventh grade at Hamilton Intermediate School this fall, but we've never been friends. Lynn and I call her Smileyface.

She whirls around in her chair, smiling like the face on a stress ball. She looks older today, dressed in a tailored black suit. Her curly red hair, which is usually gushing all over the place, is neatly coiled in a bun with a pencil sticking out of it. She looks like a real reporter. I cross my arms, hoping to cover Jason's drool on my T-shirt.

"It's so awesome working here as an intern." She plays with the plastic badge that hangs from a cord around her neck. It says "STAFF" in big letters. "Tonight, there's an opening party at the museum. I'm invited because I'm staff." She points to the badge and begins to trace the letters with her fingers. "The mayor will be there." *S.* "And Rose DeLancy, the millionairess." *T.* "She's goes all over the world buying art." *A.* "It's going to be great." *F.* "I can't wait." *F.*

I can't help thinking that it should be me meeting the mayor and Rose DeLancy at that party. I had filled out an application to be an intern, but since Dad had to zip off to Germany to sort out this big merger, Mom thought it would be better if I stayed home to help her with Jason. I actually want to be there to show Jason the fun side of life, but I know I could have juggled being an intern, too.

Cynthia gives Jason back to me. "Gotta run," she says. "Look after your mother for us. She looks like she's having a rough time. I hope your father will get back soon."

I nod. I smell Filipe and whirl around, hoping to catch his attention.

"Hi, Filipe," says Anne Marie, smiling. "Let's talk again real soon. I loved your story about the soccer match. It was so educational."

Educational, I bet. "I'd like to hear it too," I tell him.

"Oh, gross, what is that disgusting smell?" says Anne Marie, sniffing. Filipe looks at me and backs away, fanning the air.

I realize Jason has just let out a big, nasty-smelling poop. I bolt to the bathroom. *Thank you very much, Jason.*

I change his diaper. "I know you have to poop," I say, "but could you not do it around Filipe?" Jason gurgles. I put on extra baby lotion, so he'll smell nice, but when I come out, Filipe is gone. Mom is leaning over Anne Marie's shoulder. I get this icy feeling.

"We can use that," says my mother. "You're so organized and detail-oriented."

"I'm learning from the best," gushes Anne Marie.

Wouldn't they be the perfect fact-filled mother-daughter team?

Jason fidgets. I walk him around, bouncing him a little. He likes that. "I should have that job and not her," I whisper to Jason. "I would find more than facts. I think newspaper articles should be interesting, as well as factual."

Anne Marie has a smile pasted to her face while she stares up at my mother. I picture Anne Marie smiling her way through life. Until—a catastrophe! She can't stop smiling. She can't chew. She can't talk. She can't even whistle for her dog. All she can do is smile. "We must operate at once," the surgeons say.

I stare at what could have been my desk. There's a stack of flyers next to Anne Marie's computer. I grab one. It has information about the Staten Island Preservation Society Fair, which Mom organizes. When I turn it over, I suck in my breath. The back headline announces a new teen writing contest, sponsored by the society. *My mother is president of the society. Why didn't she tell me about this?*

The flyer says the contest is open to anyone twelve years of age or older. This is fate—I just turned twelve. Maybe this is my lucky day.

TWO

The window seat in my bedroom is *the* spot on earth where I feel most like a writer. What a view! I can see a panorama of New York Harbor-from the Statue of Liberty to the Verrazano Narrows Bridge. I can watch the world from this seat.

The flyer says contestants will write a thirty-minute one-act play that takes place on Staten Island during the late 1800s. It will be judged not only on style but, most important, on its authentic sense of Staten Island history.

A play. Hmmmm. A play can't be much harder than a story, can it? After all, Lynn and I love acting out our favorite movies. We know *Gone With the Wind* by heart.

I lean back against the pillows and think. No, I *visualize!* I visualize winning the contest. As they announce the winner, the crowd will part. I walk, no, I saunter, maybe amble, no, I will saunter like a princess over to the stage and accept my prize. I will share the two hundred dollars with my baby brother. I'm philan-thropic. When my manuscript is read, a hush falls over the crowd. "A masterpiece!" someone shouts, and the applause is deafening.

Then, and this is the best part, my story will be published in the society's journal and displayed in their lobby for an entire year. I shall visit it daily.

At the bottom of the flyer is a registration form. I fill in my name—Sarah Olivia Simmons—giving the S's big loops so my name looks fancier. I print my address, phone number, and age.

"Hey," says Mom, popping her head in. "Jason's sleeping. He looks like an absolute angel."

"He is an angel," I say. "Dad says he takes after me."

"That's true." She comes over and kisses my cheek. "You've been a lifesaver this summer. I would be falling apart without you." She squeezes my hand. "I just got an e-mail from your father. He hopes to wrap up that merger by next week and come home to us."

"I hope so," I say.

"He sends you his love." Mom picks up the dulcimer I bought at a yard sale. It's a beautiful instrument with romantic curves and heart-shaped cutouts. A best-selling author must have interesting hobbies to share with her readers on a book's back inside flap. I haven't actually done anything interesting yet, so I thought the dulcimer might be a good start.

She plucks one of the strings. "This is very unusual."

"I know," I agree.

"I have a great idea," she says. "With the nanny

starting on Monday, I'm hoping to give you a lot more free time. Why don't I treat you to lessons?"

I shrug. "I don't think I'm ready yet. "

"Nonsense," says Mom. "You have the rest of summer vacation."

"I'll get around to it," I say. "Am I the very first to apply?" I add, holding up my application.

"Well, yes, but—" She stares at the contest registration I'm holding.

"What's wrong?" I ask. "Should I give it to someone else?" My mother isn't judging the contest. The flyer says Peter Boswin, a historian at the college, is the judge. "I'll bring it over to the college if Dr. Boswin is there."

"Sarah," says Mom. She has a pained expression on her face as she puts down the dulcimer. "I know how much writing means to you." Her tone is making me nervous. "But you can't enter this contest."

"Why not?"

"It would be unethical," she says.

"Unethical! How could it be unethical?"

She takes my hand. "It would be unethical for a member of my family to enter."

I pull my hand away. "But you're not the judge."

"It doesn't matter. It would put Peter in a very difficult position. How could he give the other contestants fair consideration when my daughter is an applicant?"

"But, Mom, his job is to pick the best writer, whoever that turns out to be."

She sighs. "Sarah, be reasonable."

"I don't want any advantages. I just want a chance like everyone else." My voice is high and scratchy. "Mom, this contest means a lot to me."

"There are other contests."

I shake my head. "Not like this one. The winner gets published in the society's journal and receives two hundred dollars. It gets read at the fair, and the manuscript is displayed in the society's showcase for a whole year. This is a big deal!"

Mom pulls at her hair. "Honey, I realize it's a great contest. I designed it to motivate young writers to improve their writing and research skills." She begs me with her eyes. "Can't you see how difficult your entering would be for me?"

I shake my head, trying to keep myself from crying.

"Honey, I'll make—" Her cell phone rings and she flips it open. "Joe, just a minute." She leans in to me. "I'll make this up to you, I promise." She leaves.

I collapse into the window seat. Mom didn't want me at the newspaper, and now she won't let me enter her contest. Why is she doing this to me?

THREE

I find a word in the thesaurus to describe my mood: *cantankerous.*

I begin a new story. A woman invents a time-travel cell phone. Hundreds of kids line up to use it, and one by one, she lets them make a call, and off they zip into the future. Her daughter tries desperately to get a turn but can't get near the phone.

I toss my notebook aside. I'm too cantankerous to write. After being cantankerous for as long as I can stand it, I do what I usually do when I'm upset. I read Antonia DeMarco.

I find *Enraptured Thorns in My Heart,* Antonia's best book. Antonia DeMarco is one of my favorite writers. She writes about great, heroic women. Mom dislikes Antonia DeMarco. She calls her a "silly romance queen." I bring the book downstairs, where it's cooler and where Mom can see what I'm reading. I sit in the living room. It's an old-fashioned room like most of the rest of the house. I sit on our burgundy velvet sofa and begin to read.

He draws near and her heart hammers away inside her chest. This is the moment Amanda has been waiting for all her wretched life. But as he hesitates before her, the question remains, will he kiss her and renounce the beautiful but artificial Celeste?

"Sarah," says Mom. "Beth and Brendan are coming over."

I continue reading. *"You look exquisite," he says.*

"Sarah, please don't be angry with me." I've never stayed angry with Mom for long, but this is different. Very different.

He caresses her hand.

The bell rings and Mom goes to the door.

She tingles at his touch. No one has ever made her feel like this.

"Sarah."

I look up. Brendan and his mother, Beth, are in the foyer.

"Aren't you going to say hi?" says Mom.

"Hi," I say, and look down at my book.

"Beth and I need to meet for a while. We have to discuss the fair." She means the Staten Island Preservation Society Fair, which includes the writing contest that *I'm not allowed to enter!*

Brendan carries in a big box and drops it next to the coffee table. I don't want to look, but I do. It's the flyers for the writing contest.

"See ya," says Brendan.

"Wait a minute," says Beth. She tucks in the front of Brendan's T-shirt, which he immediately untucks. It's another silly shirt with a drawing of an upside-down cereal bowl running away from a bloody knife. The caption underneath reads, "Cereal Killer!"

"While we have you two," says Beth, "would you be sports and take the flyers around? You know, put them up on bulletin boards, in mailboxes, on car windows?"

"We'd really appreciate it," my mother chimes in.

"You want me to hand out *this* flyer?" I'm astounded. How could she ask this of me?

"Sarah," says Mom, nudging me. "Just deliver them around the neighborhood. Afterward, you and Brendan could take a ride together and have some fun."

"I'm busy," says Brendan.

"Me too." I point to my book. Mom raises her left eyebrow when she sees it's Antonia DeMarco.

"Just do it for half an hour," says Beth. "It's for a very worthy cause." Beth hands Brendan a stack of flyers. "It will go quickly if you work together."

"Don't I have any rights?" he says in a gruff voice.

"Of course you do," says Beth. "But that doesn't mean you shouldn't help your mother for a measly half hour."

"That's all we're asking," says my mother, smiling. I know what my mother is up to. She thinks Brendan and I could be friends. She thinks she is doing something nice. She is misguided.

"Are you coming?" he asks.

I follow him. "A half hour and not a minute

longer," I call back into the living room. I can't believe I'm doing this.

"Here," Brendan hands me the flyers and walks to his bike.

"Excuse me," I say. "We're supposed to be doing this together." I pick off about half the flyers and hand them back to him. By the time I get my bike out of the garage, Brendan is already down the block.

I go from car to car and tuck a flyer under the windshield wipers. I see Brendan flinging flyers wherever he pleases, littering lawns, stuffing them in rosebushes, crumpling them, and throwing them at trees.

I pedal over to him. "It wouldn't kill you to put the flyers in the mailboxes."

"Really?" he says.

"Yes, really."

I get off my bike. "See, it only takes a second to do it the right way." I slip the flyer in the mailbox.

"Wow," he says, grinning. "That only took a second, princess."

Great! Now he's making fun of me. How can Lynn think he's cute and sweet? But she also thinks orange is a great color and that Jane Austen is a better writer than Antonia DeMarco.

We, or shall I say *I*, continue to distribute flyers. Brendan flings a few more flyers and then tosses the rest into the corner garbage can. He rides alongside me without holding the handlebars, just leaning back with his arms crossed, watching me work.

I picture Brendan wearing one of those black-and-white striped prison uniforms with a cap to match. I will escort my mother to see him on visiting day. "But I thought he was such a good boy," she'd cry. "How could I have not seen what a public nuisance he is?"

"Hey," he says. "There are these two snakes living in the snake house at the zoo. One snake says to the other, 'Are we poisonous?' 'Why do you ask?' asks the other. The first snake answers, 'I'm a little worried because I just bit my lip.'"

He laughs at his own joke. "Don't you find that funny?"

"Snakes don't have lips."

"You really should work on getting a sense of humor," he says. We pedal on. Brendan rides with the front wheel up. You'd never know that we're the same age. It's embarrassing to be with him.

I distribute more flyers. Brendan rides in circles, getting in my way.

"Hey," he says. "I rode all the way to South Beach in fifteen minutes."

"Wow," I say in my dumbest voice. "In only fifteen minutes."

"Very funny," he says. "But don't be surprised when I make it into the *Guinness Book of World Records*."

"Really. For what? Long-distance annoyance?"

"You definitely need a sense of humor," he says.

"And you definitely need a clue." Yawn. Why couldn't I have an interesting adversary? Like someone from Antonia's books. Her men are handsome and exotic like Filipe Santo. They argue about sophisticated things.

"You're a conceited snob," says Brendan. "That's another reason you couldn't be a princess."

Antonia's men are mature and well educated.

"If you really were as great as you think you are, then you'd be able to ride to South Beach in less time than I can."

Antonia's men know how to talk to a woman.

Brendan leans in. "Well, of course, if you can't do it, I understand."

I push him away. "If I wanted to ride to South Beach, I'd get there in twelve minutes."

He leans in again. "Prove it."

"I'm busy."

He grabs the flyers from my hand, rides to the curb, and tosses them into the nearest garbage can. "Not anymore."

"You have a lot of nerve!" I ride to the garbage can. The flyers are in reach, but I stare at them. The side announcing the contest is faceup. Why should everyone be allowed to enter that contest but me? Antonia's women are bold. Antonia's women have power over their lives. I check my watch. One-fifteen. "You're on!"

I'm flying down the street. The breeze feels great.

"You'll never make it in twelve," yells Brendan, gaining to my right.

I pedal as if my life depends on it.

FOUR

As we near the beach, I taste the delicious salt air. There is nothing like the beach. I ride onto the boardwalk and screech to a halt. My watch reads 1:26. "Yes!" I yell. "Eleven minutes."

"Hey," says Brendan, pulling up beside me. "What's gotten into you? You were riding like me." He looks at his watch. "Let's see. Was that thirteen minutes and ten seconds?"

"Eleven minutes," I gloat. It's not like I've won the Tour de France, but it's something.

"Sarah Simmons, is that you?" Lucy's mother walks up the beach ramp, waving. "Lucy is having a great time at camp. Says she's becoming a real tennis pro." She smiles. "How's your summer?"

"It's great. I have a new brother."

"Wonderful." Mrs. Feldon pats my shoulder. "Hi, Brendan. Have to run."

"Say hi to Lucy," I call after her.

"Hey." Brendan nudges my arm. "What did the fish say when it got caught in the seaweed?"

I shrug.

"Kelp! Kelp!" he says, laughing.

I ride away, pumping the pedals. I'm thinking of Lucy at tennis camp. She's so lucky to have a mother who encourages her to do what she likes.

I love the *rrrrrrrr* my tires make as they push against the boardwalk. Brendan rides alongside.

"Hey!" he says. "Why are fish well educated? Because they travel in schools."

"Ah," I say.

"What is with you?" he asks. "I'm giving you some of my best jokes."

"I guess I'm not in a good mood."

"You're telling *me.*"

I slow down and breathe in the ocean air and try to catch the mist on my tongue. I listen to the waves crash. A seagull swoops by.

Brendan stares at the beach. "We should go swimming."

I feel the rhythm of the waves. I'd love to go swimming. "If we had planned on coming here, I would have brought my suit."

"Who needs a suit?"

I blush. He couldn't possibly mean go swimming in the nude. Could he? He gets off his bike, walks it down the ramp and across the sand. He leaves it resting on its side, its front wheel still spinning. He takes off his sneakers, socks, and T-shirt, runs into the water and jumps up as the waves crash against his chest. He's a lot more muscular than he used to be.

Last night Lynn e-mailed saying Brendan is not only cute, but also sexy. "Don't take offense," she wrote, "but I know about these things." She had a boyfriend for three weeks, but I don't think that makes her an authority.

I guide my bike along the same path Brendan took and leave it next to his. I take off my shoes and socks. Maybe I'll just put my feet in the water. I walk along the sand and my feet sink in. I step over shells and bits of seaweed. A woman is making a sand castle with her son and daughter. I can't wait to do that with Jason.

"Hey, come on," calls Brendan, waving to me.

"I can't swim in my clothes." The beach is crowded with people sunning themselves, reading, or sleeping under umbrellas. There's this mysterious woman dressed all in black who seems to be hiding behind her umbrella. Is she crying? I take a step closer, wishing I had my notebook with me.

Brendan grabs my arm and pulls me in. "Don't be a wimp. Your clothes will dry."

"I'm not a wimp," I say, but my voice is drowned out by a wave crashing over my head. It's cool and wonderful. A group of kids are body surfing. Brendan swims out a bit to where it's not so crowded, and I follow.

"What were you doing back there?" he asks.

"Watching someone," I say.

"You watch too much. You should *do* more."

We float on our backs, gazing at the clouds. This is so peaceful. I look at Brendan. He's staring at me. I look at the clouds again.

He splashes water at me. "I've just decided that I'm not helping our mothers with the fair this year."

Lucky him.

"And how about you?"

I swish the water around. "I don't have a choice."

"Everyone has a choice. Stand up to your mother. Just say no. Do you want to spend the rest of the summer selling raffle tickets and handing out flyers?"

I shake my head. "Absolutely not."

"Then do something about it. If you say no and I say no, then we'll have strength in numbers. It's the only way. Be strong. Say no to selling raffle tickets."

"I'll try," I say.

"Try very hard. Isn't there something else you'd rather be doing?"

"Yes," I say. "But Mom won't let me do it."

"What is it?" he asks.

"Entering the teen writing contest." I sigh. "I know I'd win."

"Then you have to enter," he says. "Don't let her stop you."

"What good will it do? Once Mom sees my name, she'll disqualify me."

"It's simple," he says. "Use a different name."

• • •

Brendan leaves to meet his friend Steve. But I can't get his idea out of my head. It's so bold, so exciting, so Antonia DeMarco. I pass the arcade, the ball fields, and the old men playing bocci ball. What if I win? Would Mom be fired as president of the Preservation Society? Will she ever speak to me again? Or would anyone care besides my mother? If a person really, really wants something, shouldn't she pursue it? What a confusing decision! If only Lynn weren't so far away.

Besides, who would I be? Victoria is a name I've always liked. It sounds like a writer. Antonia—Victoria. Very similar. I try a few last names. Victoria Summers. Victoria Winters. Or I could use Lynn's last name and make it Victoria Johnson. It's not as romantic sounding as Summers or Winters, but Johnson might bring me luck. I compromise and decide on Victoria Winters Johnson. It makes me sound mysterious.

I ride home feeling happy for the first time in a long time. I should be able to come up with a plot by this evening because I have notebooks filled with ideas. I never have a problem finding something to write about. The only problem I have, and I hate to admit this, is that by the time I get halfway through a story, I start to lose interest and my mind is on to another story. I have a problem with endings. Does that mean I could never be a real writer? No, I won't let that happen.

Mom is feeding Jason in the living room. She looks so content, so happy. I think back about a year when she and Dad told me that they were having another baby. I was thrilled, and I think they were a little relieved that I was happy.

I remember Dad saying that when he and Mom were trying to make the decision, there were a lot of reasons not to have another baby: Mom's job, Dad's promotion, more expenses, how I might feel. But in the end, he said, they decided to go ahead and have another baby, knowing that our family has always chosen to accept challenges with bravery, compassion, and strength. My father is one of the smartest people I know.

I know I must be brave and strong—and enter the contest!

FIVE

y brain hurts from thinking. It's been two days since
I decided to be bold and I haven't come up with a
single idea for the contest. Yesterday I went to the
library and flipped through a few books on Staten Island
history. It's mostly about farming. I made a few notes,
but I have no story line. I rode around on my bike to all
of Staten Island's most historical places, like Richmond
Town Restoration, the Alice Austen House, and Snug
Harbor Cultural Center. I didn't find anyone interesting to write about. If only a princess or some other royal
person had lived here. I'm vexed, exasperated, per-
turbed, anxious, frustrated, agitated, disheartened, and
thirsty!

I go downstairs for lemonade. Mom and Beth are
meeting again about the Preservation Fair. Peter
Boswin, the judge of the writing contest, is sitting on my
living room sofa. Most of the time, Dr. Boswin looks
half asleep, like his mind is off wandering the shelves of
the Library of Congress, but today he actually looks ani-

mated. Mom is talking in that I-won't-accept-anything-but-what-I-want tone. I slip into the kitchen and pour lemonade into a glass. Next to the refrigerator is an opened box packed with raffle tickets. I kick the box. I will say no to selling them. I am Victoria Winters Johnson and I am going to write a bold and fabulous historical play, if it kills me.

The front door shuts with a bang. Seconds later, the kitchen door flies open. Mom marches in, followed by Beth.

"I cannot believe that Peter would do this to us," says my mother. "He had to have known about it for weeks. He should have told me about it sooner."

"Finding a replacement took time," says Beth.

Mom rummages through papers on the table, desperately looking for something. "What's going on?" I ask Beth.

"Peter can't judge the teen writing contest," she says. "He's been funded to do research in Tuscany and he's leaving tomorrow."

Mom punches in some numbers on her cell phone. "Hi, Laura. It's Helen. Can I speak with Brian?"

"But Peter found a replacement," says Beth.

"We need someone who is used to dealing with serious literature, not fluff," says my mother. "This is the first year of the contest and its reputation will depend on how this judge handles it."

"She's a very popular writer," says Beth.

"Don't make me laugh. Brian, hi, it's Helen. I need to ask a huge favor. . . ."

"Who did he find as a replacement?" I whisper to Beth.

"Antonia DeMarco!" she says.

"Antonia DeMarco," I repeat. "*The* Antonia DeMarco!"

Beth nods. "Your mom doesn't think she's qualified."

"Mom," I say, pulling on her arm. She shoos me away.

"Mom," I say even louder. "Antonia is perfect for the contest."

She turns away from me. "Oh, I didn't know you were moving, Brian. Of course, I understand. I'll find someone else." She clicks off the phone and goes back to her stack of papers.

"Mom, Antonia DeMarco is a great writer!"

Mom pulls at her hair. She has more spikes than ever. "There are lots of good writers in New York City who would be very happy to work with young talent," she mumbles. "I'll be darned if I have to settle for a silly romance writer. I've heard she's impulsive, irreverent, and irresponsible."

"People exaggerate when it comes to celebrities," I say. "I'm sure she's wonderful. She's such a good writer."

"I have to find someone else."

"Helen," says Beth. "Who else could we find at this late date? Why don't you stop driving yourself crazy and

just use DeMarco. She's a big name. She'll attract people to the fair. After all, it is a fund-raiser. That's the
bottom line."

"Right," I say. "How did Dr. Boswin get Antonia
DeMarco to agree?"

Mom looks up. "She was a student of Peter's. He
was her mentor and they've kept in touch."

"Dr. Boswin and Antonia are friends? A great
writer and a boring historian! It doesn't make sense."

"Totally illogical," says my mother. "Only it's a
boring writer and a great historian."

We glare at each other.

"I like them both," says Beth. We glare at her.
"She'll draw a crowd. We could use that."

"Beth is right," I say. "She'll attract lots of people
and that will raise a lot of money for the Preservation
Society. Isn't that what you want?"

"If only Peter had told me this a month ago," says
Mom, pacing.

"Go with DeMarco," says Beth.

"I don't have a choice." Mom collapses in a chair.

If I write a play, Antonia DeMarco will read it. If
Antonia is anything like the women she writes about,
then my play will be read by someone who isn't afraid to
fantasize or be frivolous. Someone who would understand the way I write. This is fate. How could I lose? I go
to my room. I won't budge until I have written a masterpiece.

SIX

At five-thirty, Jason has us both up. Since sleep isn't going to happen, I use the time wisely by practicing how I will introduce myself to Antonia. "Hi. I just love your books. They are filled with romance, passion, and intrigue. You're my favorite writer."

I look in the mirror and pretend my reflection is Antonia. I smile sophisticatedly. Well, sort of. I will have to work on developing a more sophisticated look.

I grab my big straw hat. From the book jackets, I can tell Antonia is a hat person—just like me. She wears big, floppy ones. I just know I'm going to like her. We'll be kindred spirits. Maybe I'll invite her in for tea. Many of her characters have tea parties. I'll make cucumber sandwiches.

The only problem will be my mother. I plop on the bed and toss my hat aside. My mother is going to ruin everything. She won't be able to help herself. She is going to embarrass me in front of Antonia. Now I really have something not to sleep about.

I go downstairs, where Mom is nursing Jason. She

looks tired and worn out. "Sorry about the baby keeping you up," she says softly.

"It's okay." Jason has finally quieted down and the silence feels good. I sit on the sofa and pick up Antonia's book from the coffee table. I open it to the back inside flap. She has such a warm smile and a round, pleasing face. Her wavy chestnut hair cascades from under the big, floppy hat. How could Mom not like her?

Mom sees the book and groans. "I really wish I didn't have to work with her," she says. "I've heard that she can be very difficult."

"She's only going to read the plays," I say. "How difficult can that be?"

She winces. "Peter says she can be very demanding. Just what I need when I'm going back to work."

I suddenly have a great idea—a way to keep Mom and Antonia far from each other. I choose my words carefully. "Since you think Antonia's so difficult and since you're going to be very busy, I thought maybe I could help you deal with Antonia."

"What did you have in mind?"

"I could make sure she reads the plays by the deadline. And if she's demanding, I could do whatever has to be done. I'd be her personal assistant. You could just concentrate on your job and the fair."

"That's a fabulous idea," says my mother.

"It is?" My heart pumps faster.

"Yes. With going back to work next week, I won't

have time to supervise Antonia and the fair. I want her to take this contest seriously."

"I can make her take it seriously," I say.

Mom yawns. "I'll let her know that you'll be her assistant."

Me! Antonia's assistant!

"Promise me that you will come straight to me if there's any problem."

"Of course, but there won't be any." I'm so clever. I glide back to my room and look in the mirror. "I'll handle that. I'm Ms. DeMarco's personal assistant." I will help her organize the contest. I will attend to her every need. I'll keep Antonia and Mom as far away from each other as possible.

My destiny is getting better every minute.

SEVEN

It's stifling in my room and it's only 10:30 A.M. What a horrible time for my air conditioner to stop working. For days now, I have been trying to come up with a plot for my play. I've been successful only in driving myself crazy.

I hear voices in the foyer below. Mom calls my name and I slouch lower in my window seat. Jason is sleeping, and Mom wouldn't dare raise her voice. The nanny is supposed to drop by today and it's probably her. I'm not budging from my room until I've written at least another page. The deadline to hand in manuscripts is next week.

So far, all I've written is the beginning of a scene between two Staten Island farmers fighting over property lines. It seemed like a good idea last night, but this morning, I find nothing exciting about acreage and I can't imagine anyone else finding it exciting either. I delete the entire scene.

If only this were a fiction contest. Then I'd write about a girl living a dreary life as a farmer's daughter until the day she finds out that she is really the long-lost daughter of the king of Romania.

I lean back and look out at New York Harbor. A hundred years ago, there had to be tall ships passing by, maybe even pirate ships. What did pirates want? Treasure. Maybe one of the farmers has treasure buried on his land and he doesn't know it, but his neighbor does . . . or maybe the neighbor is a pirate himself . . . or he's in cahoots with the pirates. I love the word *cahoots*.

I spring up, pull open the closet door, hoping to find my father's old tuxedo shirt that I used to play around in. It's scrunched up like a ball on the floor. I unravel it. It's billowy and long—perfect for a pirate. I put it on over my tank top and tuck it into my shorts so the shirt billows in grand pirate style.

I spin around and stare at my reflection. It's not quite right yet. I find my old sailor hat under the bed and tuck in most of my hair. Under the junk on my desk, I find a ruler and brandish it in the air.

"Aha, Farmer Brown," I say. "I've come for me treasure and I'm not leaving without it." I begin a mock sword fight. "En garde!" I say, leaping at the farmer. As I'm doing this, the door to my room pops open. I freeze. Mom and some girl gape at me.

"Playing dress-up, I see," says the girl in an English accent. She giggles.

I'm mortified. My mother has embarrassed me in

front of a stranger. We've talked about her walking in on me. I've even begged to have a lock put on the door.

"Why didn't you knock?" I ask.

"I did," says Mom. "I guess you didn't hear me."

I turn to the girl. "Let me get one thing straight. I am not playing dress-up. I happen to be working on an idea for a story. I am a writer." I turn to my mother. "Who is she?"

Mom gives me a wary look. "This is Georgina. Our new nanny."

"What?" Georgina couldn't be more than a few years older than I am.

I throw off my makeshift pirate outfit and follow Mom and Georgina into the nursery. It bothers me that this girl thinks I'm playing dress-up like a little kid. I'm a serious writer.

"Uh, Georgina," I begin.

"Shhh," says Mom as she points to Jason, who is still sleeping.

Georgina smiles. "He's a love," she whispers. "I'm going to adore being with him."

Mom smiles back radiantly.

We tiptoe down the stairs to the kitchen. "Basically, he's a good baby," says my mother.

"Naturally," says Georgina.

"Georgina," I say. "I want you to be clear that I wasn't playing dress-up."

"I know, you've already told me." She smiles, but it's not the kind of genuine smile that tells me she understands.

"How old are you?" I hadn't planned on that question popping out yet.

"I'm twenty-five." She smiles again. Mom gives me an annoyed look.

As she saunters across the kitchen to look out the window, I'm amazed at how cool she looks on such a hot morning. She's wearing an aqua shirt that sets off her blue eyes. Georgina is beautiful and graceful.

"What a gorgeous view of New York Harbor," she says. "In fact, this whole house is fabulous."

"We've put a lot of hard work into it," says my mother. "Would you like some iced tea?"

"Yes, please," says Georgina. "If you love old homes, you must come to England." As she passes by, I get a whiff of roses. It's her perfume. It has a gentle garden smell.

Mom takes out two glasses and begins pouring.

"Where in England are you from?" I say, knowing this is a good question.

"Camden Town," she says. "It's just north of London."

I nod, pretending I've heard of the place. There's something mysterious about Georgina.

"Have you really been a nanny before?" I ask.

"Oh, yes," she answers. She sits at the table. "I've

been watching over babies all my life." She crosses her legs and smiles at my mother.

"I see. Did you bring references?"

"Of course."

Mom gives me a cross look. "Sarah, have you cleaned the bathroom like I asked you?"

"Not yet, Mom. I was working on a story." I sit next to Georgina. "Have we seen your references?"

"Sarah," says Mom, "I've already interviewed Georgina. Maybe you should start cleaning before it gets too late. We have to visit Nana Elsie soon."

Mom hands Georgina a glass of iced tea and keeps the other. She sits.

I'm bursting to find out things about Georgina, but I march upstairs. There is definitely something mysterious about Georgina. For one thing, she's too pretty to be a nanny. She should be on the cover of a magazine or gliding down a runway. I spray the tub and begin scrubbing it.

I should be concentrating on my play but I don't feel like writing about pirates anymore. It seems silly now. Am I ever going to come up with a plot?

I finish the tub, clean the sink and the toilet, and dust the picture frames and around the doorframe. I smile at the *S* etched into the doorframe. Mom found out that the initial belonged to Suzanne Anderson, a young girl who lived in our house more than one hundred years ago.

I trace the *S* with my index finger. *S* for *Suzanne*. *S* for *Sarah*. Was Suzanne like me? I don't know a lot about her, just a few facts, like her father, Captain Anderson, died on a voyage to the Caribbean.

While I'm sweeping, I visualize Suzanne sweeping this exact room on the morning her father has left for a long voyage. Was she worried about ever seeing him again? I think about this drama, and suddenly, I wonder why I've been looking all over town for a character when there's an interesting one in my bathroom.

Finally, a good idea! I type my thoughts into my laptop. Then I jump up and run to the closet, looking for the Victorian dress I wore to last year's fair. It's similar to something Suzanne would have worn. When I find the dress, I pull it over my shorts and tank top. I spin around and stare at my reflection. I spin around again, letting the skirt twirl in the air. I'm so absorbed that it takes me a moment to realize I have company.

Mom and Georgina are standing in the doorway. It's an instant replay. I hold my arms in front of me like a shield. I can't believe that this has happened to me twice in one day.

EIGHT

I turn up the volume on my CD player to drown out the world. Actually, to just drown out Georgina, who is downstairs singing to my brother. Besides being beautiful, she has a great voice. It's so annoying.

It's almost noon and beginning to get too hot to think. Mornings are best to write—that's when I feel most like a writer. If only the morning could last all day.

Yesterday, I went to the library to find information about Suzanne. All I found was a record of her engagement to a Civil War lieutenant named Richard Philips. Need to find out more info.

I begin to read the scene out loud. My play takes place in 1862. The Civil War is raging. Suzanne's family is facing financial ruin. Many of the shipping routes are dangerous because of Confederate raiders. In Scene Three, Suzanne has caught the maid, the beautiful, sophisticated, coordinated Gabriella, stealing the household money.

I walk to the window in a huff because Suzanne is mad at the maid. I sit down, trying not to wrinkle her dress. I find myself needing to wear the Suzanne dress whenever I'm writing the play. It helps me get into the mood of the Victorian period. I wonder if Antonia does this as well. Perhaps I will ask her tomorrow.

"Sarah." Georgina bursts into my room. She lowers the volume on my CD player. "This is too loud." She looks at my dress and smirks. "Playing dress-up again, I see."

"I told you, I'm working."

"Oh, sorry. Your mum called. She asked me to remind you to sell raffle tickets today."

"I didn't hear the phone ring," I say.

"I'm not surprised, with the music that loud."

Georgina grabs my favorite straw hat and puts it on. "Lovely," she says. "Might I borrow this?"

"I'm using it for one of my characters," I say.

"Perhaps after you've finished your story." She tilts my hat back and admires herself in the mirror. I hate to admit that she looks good in my hat. It takes all my willpower not to snatch it off her head.

"Would you be a love and pick up some Pampers when you go out to sell the tickets?" She takes off my hat and tosses it onto the bed. "Let me know if you change your mind about letting me wear that hat. Maybe we could make a trade for a day, if you fancy something of mine." From down the hall, Jason cries. "I'd better see to the baby," she says, leaving.

Didn't I just buy some Pampers yesterday? I think I

did. And I don't remember the phone ringing. This is all very mysterious. Is there a reason Georgina wants me out of the house?

I change and go downstairs. I don't intend to sell any raffle tickets, but I grab a ticket book as a ruse, a ploy, a clever cover.

"Oh, Georgina," I say, waving the tickets. "I'm going out."

She nods. "Tootles."

"Tootles," I answer. I'll sneak back in ten or fifteen minutes. That should give her enough time to begin whatever mysterious thing she's up to.

I walk to the end of the block and turn the corner, feeling very much like a spy. I avoid making the first left, even though my feet naturally want to turn. That's Lynn's street. I sigh, trying not to think about how much I miss her. I fan myself with the book of raffle tickets. It's unbelievably hot.

"Hey!" Twenty feet away, Brendan is coming toward me, carrying a basketball and wearing a T-shirt that reads "I can only please one person a day and today isn't your day. Tomorrow doesn't look good either." He eyes the raffle tickets I'm carrying. "You've got to be kidding. You promised you weren't going to sell any. I knew you'd weaken."

"I'm only pretending to sell them." I try passing him, but he dribbles the ball and blocks my path.

"Let's play horse."

"What in the world is horse?"

"It's a two-person basketball game. I need to practice my shooting and you need to get your mind off those stupid tickets."

"I don't play basketball."

He dribbles the ball some more, behind his back and then between his legs. "How come?"

"How come what?"

"How come you don't play basketball? It's fun."

"I don't know. I never learned."

"That's terrible. I'll teach you."

"I have to go."

"To do what? Sell raffle tickets! I won't let you."

"I'm not selling them," I say, waving the tickets. "This is just an excuse to get me out of the house. Actually, I'm in the middle of spying on someone."

His eyebrows arch upward. "Who?"

"Can't tell you."

"You must be lying then." He spins the ball on his fingertip.

"I am not."

"Don't believe you."

He drives me nuts. "I'm spying on Georgina, Jason's nanny. She wants me out of the house and I'm going back to see what she's up to."

"Interesting," he says.

"So, as you can see, I'm too busy to play basketball. I have to get back," I say, turning.

He throws the ball into his yard. "I'll come with you. You might need a witness."

I might need a witness. "All right," I say. As we walk to my house, I worry that Georgina might not be doing anything mysterious.

We creep up the porch steps one at a time. I hear music. We crouch down at the front window and look into the living room through a slit in the drapes. Georgina is moving around the room. She has pushed the coffee table to the side and rolled up the rug. How rude! Doesn't she know how old and expensive our furniture is?

"Your mother would be mad," says Brendan. "But I like the sloppy look."

"Shhh," I say, looking back into the room. Jason is propped up in his baby seat, staring up at Georgina as she moves around in her bare feet. She's not just moving, she's doing some kind of dance. It isn't ballet, but more like an abstract modern dance. She's changed her clothes, too. She's wearing a sleeveless black leotard with a thin black wraparound skirt. Her long blond hair is pulled up in a bun. She looks stunning.

"Wow, she's pretty!" says Brendan.

I poke him with my elbow. "Shhh."

Georgina seems totally lost in her dance. She glides and turns with ease and abandon. I feel like I'm watching a professional. It's amazing how well every part of her body moves in harmony with the rest. I wonder how it feels to dance like that. So uninhibited. So coordinated. So daring. So beautiful!

I turn and see Brendan staring, mesmerized. I bet he'd ask her out if he had the chance.

"I've seen enough," I say, pulling him away.

NINE

"It's not a crime to be a dancer," Brendan says as we walk down Merrit Street.

I hate to admit it, but it's not. I expected to find Georgina stealing or doing something illegal. Not dancing. "Why would she have to practice in secret?"

"Something fishy is going on," he says.

"You really think so?" I say, turning.

"I do."

"What could it be?"

"I don't know. I'm too hungry to think." We turn onto Forest Avenue, and when we get to Sal's Pizzeria, Brendan walks in. I follow him. I inhale the enticing aromas of fresh tomato sauce, melted cheese, pepperoni, garlic, and onion. Brendan orders two slices of pepperoni pizza.

"Hey, do I see raffle tickets?" asks Sal.

"Huh?" I say. I look down. I'm holding the book of tickets.

"I really enjoyed the gourmet basket I won last year. I feel lucky again. I think I'll buy a whole book."

"Stop with those things," says Brendan, sounding annoyed. Sal fishes through his wallet for money.

"I'm not selling them," I say defensively.

"You're not selling raffle tickets?" asks Sal. "Like, how come? You always sell raffle tickets."

"Because," I say. "I'm not."

Brendan nods. "That's right. She's not. Two Cokes, Sal."

"Thanks," I say, surprised by the treat.

"I'm thirsty," he says. "They're both for me."

I should have known.

We sit down at a table. Brendan slides one of the Cokes in front of me. "I guess I'm not as thirsty as I thought."

I smile and take it. He offers me a slice by pushing it in front of me. "I guess I'm not as hungry as I thought, either."

"Thanks." I'm amazed. Brendan begins eating. I stare into his deep brown eyes as I wait for my slice to cool. "Why would Georgina be working as a nanny when she's such a good dancer?"

He swallows and wipes his mouth with a paper napkin. He has dimples. "Maybe she didn't think your mother would hire her to look after your brother if she was a dancer."

I nod. "My mother is very closed-minded." As I sip my Coke, I wonder what it would feel like to touch his honey-colored hair. I nibble on my slice.

He continues, "Maybe she does want to be a nanny, but she also wants to be a dancer. Maybe she can't make up her mind. People do that all the time. They're not like me. I know what I want to be."

"What?" I ask.

"A stand-up comic."

I laugh. "What?"

He leans in; one side of his mouth turns up when he smiles. "See, I'm a natural, and you're a hard audience."

"Your mom will never let you do that."

He throws down his napkin. "It's not her choice, is it?"

I've said something wrong.

"I don't care what she says. I'm not going to be a doctor like her or a lawyer like everyone else in the family. I want to tell jokes and make people laugh. She's forbidden me to even think about being a comic. She's got a lot of nerve."

I nod. "Our moms are totally impossible."

"Totally." He bows his head. "All my life, my mother has made me do things I don't want to do. She never asks me what I want. When I try to tell her, she doesn't listen. My opinion on my own life isn't important. You should know, look at all the times she made us play chess together when we could have been hanging out with our friends."

"That wasn't right," I agree. I don't mention how

annoyingly long it always took him to make a single move.

"And going on vacations together," he adds.

"So annoying."

"I wasn't allowed to ride my bike without having you follow me everywhere I went."

"I didn't follow you!" The lady at the next table gives me a look, and I lower my voice. "Mom said I had to stay with you."

"You could never keep up."

"How could I? You ride like a maniac."

"And you ride like a girl."

We stare at each other.

"It's pretty obvious," he says, "that our mothers are clueless and we're never going to be friends."

"Totally obvious," I say. I pull on a piece of melted cheese, not wanting to look at his face. I shouldn't feel hurt. I should be glad he feels the same way I do.

"I'm not going to let my mother push me around anymore," he says.

"That's good."

"In fact"—he looks around—"I just signed myself up for the next open mike at the Java Café."

"The coffee house in Stapleton?"

"That's the one." He leans back.

"Wow." I'm impressed. "Aren't you scared?"

"I overcome my fears." He leans in. "A man walks into a doctor's office with a pelican on his head. 'You need help immediately,' says the doctor. 'I certainly do,' says the pelican. 'Get this man out from under me.'"

I laugh, probably more because of Brendan's delivery than because of the actual joke. There is definitely something funny about him, now that I'm really listening. And we have something in common—getting past our mothers. It's too bad we can't be friends.

"Hey, another patient says, 'Doctor, I broke my arm in two places!' And the doctor says, 'Stay out of those places!'"

"How about this one," he says. He starts a joke about a farmer and a pig, but I'm staring at the woman talking to Sal. She's wearing this dramatic-looking black skirt with gold embroidery on it. Her arms are covered with bracelets that jingle as she moves. She's also wearing a large, floppy hat so I can't see her face, but she reminds me of a movie star. I hear a snippet of their conversation.

"I'm in the mood for something a little more exotic," she says. "I've just returned from Tokyo, you see, and I have a yen for shiitake mushrooms. Do you carry them?"

"Look, lady," says Sal. "I get my mushrooms from a supply house."

She waves her arms and the bracelets jingle. "I highly recommend you order shiitake mushrooms. Your customers will be thrilled."

"Do you want a slice or not?"

She looks at the various pies and shakes her head.

"Next!" yells Sal.

The movie-star lady turns around. She has a pretty, round face and it looks familiar. I wonder where . . . Oh, it can't be! "Do you know of a restaurant that serves shiitake mushrooms?" she asks, staring directly into my eyes. I can name three Japanese restaurants, but my mouth isn't working.

"Never heard of them," says Brendan. "What did the female mushroom say about the male mushroom? He's a real fun guy." He looks at her and laughs. "Don't you get it? *Fun guy,* fungi."

"Ah, yes, funny," she says without laughing. She turns to leave.

"It was a good one," Brendan calls after her. "Here's a real funny one. What did one cannibal say to the other cannibal—"

"Omigod," I say, almost knocking over my Coke. "It's *her.*"

"Who?" asks Brendan. "Why isn't anyone laughing at my jokes?"

I don't have time to answer. I'm running out the door. I see Antonia DeMarco cross the street. I start after her from the middle of the block. A horn blows and I freeze. I turn to see a red car coming at me. A hand grabs me from behind and pulls me onto the sidewalk.

"Are you trying to get yourself killed?" Brendan yells.

My knees feel shaky. "I was just following Antonia DeMarco." Brendan is holding me. "I'm her assistant." I know I should run or I'll never find her, but just then, Brendan pulls me closer and suddenly we kiss. I feel dizzy, confused. Before I know it, I'm running down the street, away from Brendan.

TEN

The minute my mother gets home, she knocks on my door. She tries to open it but can't because I've jammed a chair against it. "Are you okay?"

"I'm fine."

Pause from the other side. "Georgina said you were acting strange."

I can tell you a few things about *her*, I mutter under my breath. "I'm fine."

"We're having Chinese takeout for dinner."

"I'm not hungry."

Footsteps retreating. I'm staring out the window. I can't believe Brendan Callahan kissed me. I can't believe I ran away! That is so *not* cool.

"I ordered vegetable dumplings," says Mom, knocking again.

"I'm still not hungry."

"Georgina is staying for dinner. We could use your company."

"Maybe later," I say.

Her footsteps retreat. I can still feel the kiss. I touch

my lips, thinking they should feel the same, but they don't. They feel kissed. I bury my face in my knees. Why did I run away? He must think I'm an idiot.

The phone rings. My stomach drops. What if it's Brendan? Or his mother telling my mother that I acted like such an idiot? I yank the chair away from the door and step into the hallway. I hear Georgina's voice below. Thank goodness she answered and not my mother. I run down the stairs and through the living room. My mother, holding Jason, is heading to the kitchen. I get there just ahead of her and grab the phone. What am I going to say to Brendan's mom?

"Hello!" I can't hear what Mrs. Callahan said. "Hello," I say, louder.

"Sarah? Sarah, is that you?" It's not Brendan's mom. I start crying.

"Lynn," I gasp. "Is it really you?"

"Tell me what's going on."

I look at Georgina and my mother. They are both staring at me.

I can hear Lynn saying my name over and over again. "Calm down," I say into the phone.

"You're telling *me* to calm down. You e-mail me that you've done the stupidest thing and then you don't tell me what it is. Tell me right now what you did, or— or else."

I walk to the back door and open it. I stretch the phone cord as far as it will go, which is to the second step on the small back porch. I sit down on the step and look around. One of our neighbors, Mr. Fry, is watering his lawn. "Just a minute," I tell Lynn.

"Will you come on!" she screams.

"You don't have to yell."

"Yes, I do!"

When Mr. Fry walks to the other side of his yard, I take a deep breath. "Do you promise not to call me stupid?"

"I would never do that," she says. "Tell me."

I take another breath. "Brendan kissed me."

"Yay!" she says. "And?" I can hear the excitement in her voice.

"And I ran away."

"Are you stupid?"

"See, I knew you'd say that."

A pause, and then she says, "Lots of love stories begin that way. Look at Rhett and Scarlett. Scarlett did a lot of stupid things during the whole movie."

"I know," I say. "And then he left her at the end."

"Stop being so negative," says Lynn, back to her usual calm voice. "How do you rate the kiss?"

I play with the phone cord. "I've never been kissed before."

"It doesn't matter. Close your eyes. How did it feel?"

I close my eyes. I don't have to try hard to remember. "It felt nice."

"Nice! Kisses aren't nice. They are either wonderful or awful. So which was it? Be honest."

"What are you—the authority on kissing?"

"Yes. So tell me, was it awful?"

"No."

"Then it had to be wonderful."

"Well," I say, "yeah, it was."

"Of course, it was," she says dreamily.

I twirl the cord around my fingers. "How do I explain why I ran away?"

"Tomorrow's another day, as Scarlett would say."

"That's a big help."

"You'll think of something," she says. "I have confidence in your creativity. I'd better go. Dad's hovering. We're going to see his girlfriend in a fashion show."

"Tell me all about it."

"I will."

"I miss you."

"Miss you too. E-mail me. You'll come up with something to tell Brendan."

After she hangs up, I just sit there, watching the setting sun. I do feel better. Lynn can do that to a person.

I smile at a blue jay as it swoops down on the feeder. "Tomorrow *is* another day," I say in my best Southern twang. "I'll think about what to say to Brendan tomorrow."

ELEVEN

By morning, I've thought of a hundred ways of avoiding Brendan for the rest of my life. It's the only solution.

Mom pops her head in before leaving for work. "Before I forget"—she reaches into her pocket and hands me a piece of paper—"here's Antonia's address and phone number. You're to call her this morning. The entries are downstairs. She must begin reading them."

I grab the paper and see an address I don't recognize.

"She rented a bungalow in South Beach. She said not to call her before ten." Mom shakes her head. "If you have any problems with her, remember to tell me immediately."

I nod.

She kisses my cheek. "You're looking pale. Why don't you call Brendan and go for a bike ride together?"

"Brendan," I mutter.

"Or maybe you'd like to play chess."

"No thanks," I say. *I'd rather kiss him!* I turn away from her, not believing what I just thought.

I try to write for the next two hours, but all I can think about are Brendan's lips and what to say to Antonia. At two minutes before ten, I walk down to the kitchen. I wait three minutes and then I call Antonia. My hands tremble so much I can barely press the numbers.

The line rings four, five, six times. Finally someone picks it up.

"Hellloo," comes a mellow voice.

"Is this Antonia DeMarco?" My voice is unsteady.

A pause, then, "Who is this?"

My hand tightens around the receiver. "Hi, I'm Sarah Simmons."

"Who?" There is music in the background.

Could this be her? "I'm Helen Simmons's daughter."

Pause. I lean against the wall to steady myself. "I'm calling about the teen writing contest."

Pause.

"Contest? Oh, yes. What about it?"

"I have the plays Ms. DeMarco needs to read. I'm her personal assistant on this project."

"How lovely," she says. "I'll tell you what. I'm doing a book signing at Barrett Books today. Do you know it?"

It *is* her. "Yes," I say excitedly.

"Good," she breathes into the receiver. "It starts at noon. Meet me there."

"Noon," I say. "I won't be late."

"And would you be a love and bring several cans of Fancy Feast Savory Salmon?"

"Excuse me?"

"Ophelia simply loves it."

"Ophelia?"

"My cat, of course. See you at noon. Don't buy any cans that have dents. Ophelia is a bit finicky."

I hang up the phone. My mother might be right. Antonia is a little strange. But then, she is a great writer and probably very busy doing all those great things she writes about. She must love her cat very much. I will buy undented cans. I plan on being the best personal assistant Antonia ever had. Maybe after the contest is over, she will want me to continue.

I love that she's named her cat after one of Shakespeare's tragic heroines. It's so deep. I knew she would be exciting and wonderful. I'd better not mention anything about the cat food to my mother. She wouldn't understand.

"You seem in better spirits," says Georgina, breezing into the kitchen. "I was worried about you yesterday. You seemed even more peculiar than you usually are. Want to talk about it?"

"It was the heat. I'm better now. Thank you."

She nods and glides to the refrigerator, filling the air with her rose-scented perfume. She opens the door gracefully. As she stares at the contents of the refrigerator, her feet are actually in first position. Amazing. She must have years of dance training. Why didn't I see that before?

"Want some orange juice?" Georgina asks. I'd like to know why she's here, babysitting my brother, and not dancing. She should be dancing with a professional troupe. She's that good.

"Sure, I'd love some."

She brings the OJ to the table. "I'm pooped. I've walked your brother all over the neighborhood for an hour. He's napping now."

She fills two glasses and hands me one. She sits on one of the chairs, her legs crossed under her. Could I learn to be this graceful?

"Oh, I almost forgot." She goes into the other room and comes back with a large expandable folder. "Here," she says. "Your mum told me to give this to you. It's the entries for the contest."

I take the folder. It is heavy and bulky.

"Are you entering one of your stories?" asks Georgina.

"No," I say. "I'm not allowed."

"Too bad." She leans in. "I sense a lot of drama going on upstairs. Pity for it to go to waste."

Does she know I'm writing something secretly? She's always popping into my room, looking over my shoulder. Sometimes I get the impression she's spying on me.

I go upstairs and open the folder. The contents spill onto my bed. There are twenty-two entries with two days left before the deadline. Anne Marie's is on the top of the pile. Her play is called *For the Love of Alice*. Hmmm. Nice title. I skim the first scene. It's about Alice Austen, the photographer who lived around the turn of the last century and became famous for her awesome photos. I went to her museum just a few days ago. Why didn't I think of writing about Alice? No one will know Captain Anderson and his family. How can my characters compete with Alice Austen?

I look up at the clock. It's getting late. I can't start another play. I have to finish this one. Without looking at the other plays, I put them all back into the folder. I will finish. *Please, God.*

I turn on my laptop and slide into my window seat. I work on Scene Four. In this scene, Suzanne goes off to meet her love, Richard. He tells her that he has enlisted to fight against the Confederacy. Tomorrow morning, he will leave for training camp. Suzanne begs him not to go. Richard takes her into his arms and kisses her. It is their first kiss. It is wonderful. Richard asks her to marry him before he leaves. Suzanne agrees, even though her mother has forbidden it. Her mother thinks Richard is a silly and irresponsible person.

Suzanne hears footsteps behind her and she worries. Could it be the beautiful and graceful Gabriella spying on her? Will Gabriella tell her mother what Suzanne is about to do and ruin everything?

TWELVE

I want to wear something special for my first meeting with Antonia. Something that screams out I'm a writer, a talented and passionate writer. I settle for a long blue skirt, which flows when I move. To go with it, I choose a purple T-shirt—the color gradually changes hue as it descends to the bottom. Lynn thinks this shirt is totally cool. I hope Antonia does, too.

My hair is a mess. The humidity has made it frizz. I try combing it, but it doesn't look any better.

I practice my cool look. I invented this look last night. I tilt my head to the side and give a small, uneven smile as I look at the person I'm trying to impress from the corner of my eye. It suggests that I'm giving them my attention, but not all of it, because I have other things going on in my head. I hope it works.

At the last moment, I decide to wear the Suzanne hat.

I head to Granneli's Supermarket. The cool air inside Granneli's invigorates me. I rush around the store until I find cat food in aisle four. I never realized there were so many kinds of cat food. Fortunately, they carry Fancy Feast, but it takes me a while to locate salmon. I grab the only two undented cans on the shelf and run to the express checkout line, hoping Antonia will be satisfied with only two cans. The line moves slowly. I focus on the checkout girl, willing her to move faster. Finally, I pay for the two cans of cat food, which are unbelievably expensive, and head out into the hot afternoon.

I arrive at Barrett Books at 12:05. There is a display of Antonia's books on the center table. Quite a crowd is milling around. I don't see Antonia. Mr. Barrett, who is all decked out in a beige suit and a pale peach tie, leans against the front counter, staring nervously at the door. I walk over to him.

"Hi. Where's Antonia DeMarco?"

"That's what I'd like to know," he says in a snippy voice. "She's late and I have twenty customers lined up waiting for her to autograph their books." He turns to the girl at the register. "Did you call her, Marge?"

"Yes," she says, nodding. "There was no answer."

Mr. Barrett flutters about, greeting customers. "Just a little delay," he says. "Ms. DeMarco will be here momentarily."

I meander over to the fiction section and pretend to be looking at books, but I study the customers waiting. Anne Marie Valgetti is second in line, wearing a miniskirt that exposes her long, bony legs. She waves to me, her red hair springing all over the place. "Isn't this exciting," she says. "Imagine, Antonia DeMarco judging our little local contest. I entered."

"Yes, I know," I say. "I'm Antonia DeMarco's personal assistant for the contest."

"Really?" Anne Marie looks surprised. "I didn't know."

I practice my cool look on Anne Marie. I tilt my head and give her the small, uneven smile. "Her personal assistant. It's a very important job."

Her eyes narrow into tiny slits. "I hope Antonia comes soon. I have to get back to the newspaper, you know." She begins playing with her STAFF badge. "Is there something wrong with your neck?"

"No," I say, walking away from her.

"All right, everyone," says Mr. Barrett. "Antonia has arrived."

We all turn. Antonia DeMarco rushes in, wearing her floppy hat, and it makes me glad that I'm wearing mine. I'm mesmerized by the pattern in her long, flowing skirt. It has swirls of blue and purple, with dancing half moons and stars that match her earrings, which are dangling moon slivers. She looks like a movie star again. We're wearing the same colors. This must be fate.

Mr. Barrett leads Antonia to the table he has set up in the middle of the store. "These are for you." He gestures to a glass vase filled with beautiful yellow roses.

"Thank you." Antonia looks around at the crowd and then sits, like she's used to having all these people stare at her. I move closer, but Mr. Barrett stops me.

"Sarah, no cutting in the line. People have been waiting longer than you."

"I'm here as Antonia's assistant for the playwriting contest." He rolls his eyes and escorts the first customer to Antonia. Couldn't he have been a little impressed?

"I'm parched," Antonia says to Mr. Barrett. "I need some water, please." He nods and goes into the back room. I try to get Antonia's attention, but she's talking with the first customer, so I stand off to the side. It's unbelievable enough that I'm in the same room with her. I like the way she talks—her voice bounces along. Mr. Barrett comes back with a glass and a pitcher of water. He smiles at the customers while he fills the glass and hands it to Antonia, placing the pitcher on the table.

Antonia wrinkles her nose. "I'm so sorry. I should have been more explicit. I never drink tap water. Would you be a dear and find me some bottled water? I prefer Pelton Springs."

His smile fades. "Yes, of course."

Anne Marie is next. She straightens her STAFF badge and puts on that phony smile. "Antonia DeMarco," she says, gushing, "I'm your number one fan. I'm a writer, too, and I've just written a play, all about Alice Austen."

I won't let her charm Antonia into choosing her play. I march over to Antonia and stick out my hand. "I'm Sarah."

Antonia looks at me. "Who?"

Anne Marie shoots me an exasperated look. "You're cutting in."

I reach into the bag I'm carrying and take out a can of cat food and hold it up.

"Oh, yes." Antonia's face is all smiles. "Ophelia will be so happy. You are a dear."

I beam and hold up the accordion folder. "Here are the plays."

"Keep them for me," she says, rising. "I need to stretch my legs." She walks to the nonfiction section and beckons me with her index finger. I hurry over. "I hate book signings," she whispers. "They tire me considerably. A writer needs solitude, but my agent makes me do this. Honestly, they ask me the same question over and over again. It drives me mad." She affects a silly voice. "How do you come up with the ideas for your books?" She elbows me. "I'm glad you're to be my assistant. You seem a cut above the rest."

I've died and gone to heaven.

"Lovely hat," she says.

Mr. Barrett clears his throat and holds out a bottle of mineral water. "Ms. DeMarco, your fans are waiting."

Antonia smiles and strolls to the table. She inspects the bottle. "I suppose this will do. Thank you." She sits and turns back to me. "Wait for me, won't you? We must talk drama."

I almost fall over. She wants me to wait for her. We're going to talk drama. "Of course," I say. I would wait forever.

"How do you ever come up with those wonderful story ideas?" says Anne Marie, gushing.

Antonia and I exchange a knowing look. Wow! I glide around the store, dizzy with happiness. I enter a conversation with two older ladies who are trying to decide which of Antonia's books to buy. I recommend *Love Hath No Fury*. They thank me.

"I'm a friend of the author," I slip in, tilting my head. I'm getting a handle on acting cool. I wander over to the register and talk to Marge. I tell her I'm assisting Antonia.

"You'll have to tell me what she's really like," she says. "I'm a fan myself."

"Of course," I say, tilting, tilting, tilting.

"Is there something wrong with your neck?" she asks.

Perhaps my new look needs a little work.

Mr. Barrett buzzes around the store like a nervous fly. He slips copies of Antonia's books into customers' hands and guides them to the book-signing line. Every few minutes, Antonia waves him over and whispers something in his ear. He brings her different pens, tissues, more bottled water.

I stand to the side and watch Antonia. I love the way she leans forward to talk to the customers like she really cares about them. You'd never know from the way she's acting that she isn't enjoying this. Mr. Barrett looks thrilled with all the books he's selling.

I imagine that I am Antonia and all these people are here to see me. "How do you ever come up with such clever ideas for your stories?" they'd ask over and over again.

"Inspiration is everywhere," I answer.

Someone bumps into me from behind.

"Talking to yourself again?"

I turn. It's Brendan.

THIRTEEN

Brendan's eyes bore into me. Is he thinking about my running away yesterday? Say something. Anything. I can't. I look down at his shirt, which is covered with drawings of toads and says "Toad-al Chaos."

Beth steps between us, carrying a copy of *Enraptured Thorns in My Heart*. "Isn't this exciting? I love Antonia DeMarco." She elbows me and smiles shyly. "Maybe you shouldn't mention this to your mother."

This is too funny. "I won't tell her," I say.

Brendan starts to walk away, but Beth grabs his arm. "Hey, you two," she says. "Look at all these customers. Great opportunity to sell raffles!"

"I told you I'm not going to sell them anymore," he says. "I'm tired of annoying people with them."

"Nonsense. People love to buy raffle tickets. Right, Sarah?"

Brendan turns to me and our eyes lock. They really do. I thought that was just an expression, but I couldn't look away if I tried. I see the challenge in his stare: *Stand up for us!*

"Brendan's right. It's a tough job and we've been doing it a long time," I say, not looking away from his eyes. "Ask some of the younger kids."

I've never stood up to her before. There's a hint of a smile on Brendan's face.

"Well," Beth says, looking uncomfortable. "I suppose I should get in line." She walks away.

"You see, strength in numbers works," Brendan says.

"Strength in numbers," I repeat. I fidget with the folder I'm holding. "I'm sorry I ran away yesterday."

"You made me feel like a jerk," he says.

"No," I say, looking up. "It was stupid of me to run. Meeting Antonia made me nervous."

"Yeah, right." He puts his hand in his pocket. "Don't worry." He takes his hand out. He crosses his arms. "It won't happen again."

"Right," I say, trying to sound like I don't care. "Of course not."

"Oh, Sally." Antonia DeMarco waves her hand. I look around for a Sally but don't see anyone. She points to me.

"Excuse me, Brendan." I walk over.

"Sally, dear. I'm beginning to get hungry. Would you be a love and run to the nearest deli to get me a sandwich?"

"Of course. But my name is Sarah."

"How silly of me," she says, smiling. "I'd like tuna salad on rye bread. But without seeds. And make sure the mayonnaise is fresh. Have them add lettuce, but it must be romaine. And tomatoes, but I don't like the outside slices."

"Is that all?" I ask.

"Yes," she says. "I hate to be a bother."

"Oh, you're not," I say. "I'm your personal assistant. Anything you want."

I turn, trying to think of the closest deli.

"Oh, and one more thing, dear."

I turn back. "A diet root beer. A&W, of course."

"Of course."

I wave at Brendan. "Have to go." He nods. I find the closest deli, but they don't have rye bread without seeds. The next deli doesn't have romaine lettuce. I end up having to go to three different delis to complete her order, putting the sandwich together myself. I've taken a long time and I hope she isn't mad.

When I get back to the bookstore, Mr. Barrett is standing over Antonia, whispering in her ear. Antonia looks pale and is massaging her temples.

"I'm developing quite a headache," she says. "I don't know if I can continue."

Mr. Barrett looks around and smiles at the customers. "Just a brief delay," he says. "Ms. DeMarco will be back to signing her books in a moment."

"I have your sandwich," I say, offering it to her.

"Yes, have something to eat," says Mr. Barrett.

"Thank you," she says, opening her lunch.

I look around for Brendan. He's near the door and Anne Marie is next to him, talking and smiling, talking and smiling. I move closer. Not to make it obvious that I'm listening in on their conversation, I reach out and pull a book off the shelf. It's about golf.

I watch Brendan from the corner of my eye. I'm not trying to be cool. I'm checking to see if he's gazing lovingly into her eyes, only it's hard to tell from this distance. He laughs at something she says. I move closer. This time picking up a book on curling— whatever that is.

They are talking about some concert. "I just love the Electric Shockers," Anne Marie gushes. "Are you a fan?" Another smile.

"Yup." Brendan nods.

Yet another smile. "They're playing at the Garden on Saturday," she says.

"Wow," says Brendan. "I wouldn't mind going to that!"

I walk away because I couldn't bear to hear him ask her out. Why is it that Anne Marie always seems to be hovering around my life, taking things that belong to me? I walk back to the register, trying to recall all the things I've always hated about Brendan. Like the way he rides his bike like a maniac and his rudeness and his silly jokes. But they don't seem as real as the kiss.

Turning back, I catch Brendan and Anne Marie walking outside together, and my heart crumbles like a cookie that's been sat on.

FOURTEEN

I have a long wait for Antonia. Instead of driving myself crazy, wondering if Brendan and Anne Marie are out there kissing, I take notes. I don't want to forget this scene with its long line of adoring fans who can't keep their eyes off Antonia. I love the queenly way she sits and welcomes them and the look on their faces when they finally get to talk to her. I eavesdrop and jot down bits and pieces of conversations.

"Ladies and gentleman," says Mr. Barrett. "I must interrupt the signing for a few minutes so that Ms. DeMarco can give a short interview."

A nervous-looking woman steps forward. She studies the notes she's written on a crumpled piece of paper and clears her throat. "Hi, Ms. DeMarco," she says. "I'm from Staten Island College and I'd like to ask you a few questions for the readers of our newsletter."

"Certainly," says Antonia.

The woman smiles. "How do you come up with the ideas for your books?"

Antonia throws her head back and gives me a look. I nod understandingly. The woman rattles off questions like, "Did you always want to be a writer? Who is your favorite author?"

"Myself, of course," she answers with a laugh. "But seriously, I adore Shakespeare. I encourage everyone to read all of his plays."

During the interview, I learn a few things about Antonia that I didn't know, and I record them in my notebook. She was an orphan, raised by her aunt in Vermont; she's been married three times but still believes in love; and she's had lots of odd jobs all over the country.

About fifteen minutes later, Mr. Barrett says, "Unfortunately, we must stop the interview because Antonia has a lot more books to sign." The lady asks if Antonia will pose for the newsletter photographer, and she agrees. Mr. Barrett rushes to Antonia's side in time to be photographed with her.

Antonia signs books for another hour. About three-thirty, the line finally ends. She rises and stretches. "Where is Sally?"

I rush over. "It's Sarah," I correct her again.

She nods and puts her hat back on. "Sarah," she says grandly. "We have business to attend to, don't we?" I smile and feel a rush of excitement as she says my real name. We walk out of the store with Mr. Barrett, who is thanking her again and again. We get to her car, a convertible. When Antonia replaces her hat with a silky scarf and puts on sunglasses, she looks even more like a movie star.

I've never ridden in a convertible before. It's so cool. Wait until I e-mail Lynn.

"I need to unwind before I can take care of our contest business. I hope you understand."

I nod and she pulls away speedily from the curb, cutting off the car behind her. The driver of that car beeps the horn. I look away in case it's someone I know.

I have to hold my hat in my lap because it keeps trying to fly away.

"What is your next book about?" I ask, hoping this is a question she likes.

"Oh, that," she says, waving her hand. "I'd much rather hear about you. What are your dreams, Sarah? What are your passions?"

I blush. "I want to be a writer. I've always wanted to be one."

She turns and smiles. "Then you shall. I can sense the writer in you."

Antonia DeMarco senses the writer in *me*. She has known me for a little over three hours and yet she knows. I get goose bumps all over.

"What are you working on right now?" she asks. "Tell me about it."

I wish I could tell her about my play, but under the circumstances, how could I? "I haven't finished anything yet." I take out my notebook and read off some of my plot notes.

"You've made some good observations," she says. "Of course, I used to do the very same thing. Details. Details. That is what has made me a great writer."

I write DETAILS in my notebook. We drive up a curved road, snaking back and forth to the top of the hill as the wind blows in my hair. I point out St. Andrew's Church and its cemetery, which has tombstones dating to the mid-1600s. She pulls over and parks. We get out and walk through the graveyard.

"Look here," she says, pointing to a small marble stone with the inscription *Eliza Stubens, 1842–1847*. "She was just a little girl." We stand there staring at the stone. "What a pity," she says. "What do you think she died of?"

"Probably cholera," I say. "There was an epidemic around that time."

"How awful." Antonia presses one hand over her mouth and nods sadly. I can feel her sensitivity for poor Eliza.

"You certainly seem familiar with local history," she says.

I'm about to say my mother is a history nut, but I stop myself. I don't want to bring my mother into this perfect afternoon. We move on to other stones and read off names and dates, talking about life back then. Antonia is so easy to talk to.

"I'm getting a very good feeling from you," she says.

"Thank you," I say.

"I've been going through a rough time."

"That's terrible," I say. "Can I do anything to help?"

She stares deeply into my eyes. "Sarah, what I'm about to tell you must be kept in strictest confidence. I feel that I can trust you."

We're kindred spirits, I want to tell her.

"Please promise not to repeat what I am about to tell you."

"Your secret is safe with me," I say.

She stares straight ahead. "I'm blocked creatively."

"Oh, no," I say.

She nods. "I haven't written a thing in, well, a while. That's why I've come to Staten Island. I needed to be away from my editor, my agent, a certain Hollywood producer, and the swarms of fans. I need to think, relax, sort things out."

"Tell me what to do," I beg.

"Perhaps you can help keep my fans at bay so I can relax. There has been so much pressure to start my next book and then there's that screenplay."

I can't believe that Antonia would be creatively blocked. What if she never wrote another book? What would her fans do? What would *I* do?

FIFTEEN

"Pass the string beans," says Georgina at dinner. I do, but I'm barely aware of what is going on around me. I'm too excited.

When I got home, I wrote the last scene of the play. I really like what I wrote. This is how I ended the play: Suzanne sneaks out of the house to marry Richard. Meanwhile, her mother follows her to the church and they have a loud confrontation. Her mother forbids her to marry Richard. Suzanne is torn because she has always been an obedient girl, but Richard has made her realize he needs her. He not only loves her, he respects and cherishes her talents. She has always wanted this respect, which her mother has obviously not had for her. The play ends with Suzanne and Richard walking hand in hand into the church.

"How's work going?" Georgina asks Mom.

"I had quite a day," she says, patting Jason's back. "It's so hard being away from him." They continue to talk, but I'm thinking about Antonia. She has honored me by telling me her darkest secret. I'm the only person who knows she has writer's block. I'm the only person who can help her. This is a huge responsibility, but I must find a way.

"Sarah. Sarah, are you with us?"

"Huh?" I say.

"I said, when I got home," says my mother, "I came to your room to say hello and you didn't even hear me. You must be working hard on a story."

I hadn't noticed my mother at all. I was too busy finishing my play. I still can't believe I finally finished something. I owe it to Antonia and the confidence she has in me.

"Do you need help with your story? Remember, I promised to help you find another contest."

"No, thanks," I say. "Antonia loves working with young writers. She is the most amazing woman I have ever met."

"Oh," she says, sounding disappointed. "That's very generous of her. But I really meant it when I said I would help you. Really."

"Don't worry," I say. "I'm in good hands."

Mom shifts Jason to her other arm. "Tell us about this amazing woman."

"She's so likable, so interesting, so exotic," I say.

"Really," says Georgina. "Tell us more."

"Do tell us," says Mom.

"She rented a convertible for the day," I say. "Antonia is like that. She does creative, fun things. But the best part is how sensitive she is. She can see deeply into a person. She told me that she can sense the writer in me. Isn't that amazing, after only knowing me for a few hours?" I look right at my mother.

"Amazing," replies my mother in a very unamazed tone. "Did she bother to read anything you wrote before reaching that conclusion?"

"She doesn't have to. She understands things the average person doesn't."

"What sort of things?" asks Georgina.

"Antonia has experienced true suffering and true passion. She has deep feelings, which is why she'll be the perfect judge for the teen writing contest. She'll know which writers are really expressing deep feelings rather than just listing facts and dates."

"Speaking of the contest," says Mom, "did you give her the plays to read?"

"Of course." I left them in the backseat of her convertible, but I'm not going to tell Mom this.

"Do you think I should call her?" asks Mom. "To answer any questions she might have."

"Not necessary," I say. "That's what you have me for." Jason fidgets and begins to cry.

"I have a deep feeling that this little boy needs changing." Georgina gets up and takes Jason upstairs. "Be back in a bit."

I chew on a string bean, daydreaming about the wind blowing through my hair as Antonia and I ride around Staten Island. I must remember to wear sun-glasses and a scarf next time.

There's a knock on the back door. "I'll get it," Mom says. I bring my plate over to the sink and wash it. When I look up and see Brendan, I knock over the plas-tic container of liquid soap, and it drops to the floor, squirting soap all over the place. Brendan probably thinks I'm a dork.

Brendan doesn't look at me. He hands Mom a folder. Why isn't he looking at me? What's wrong with him? Where did he and Anne Marie go after they left the store?

"This is from my mother."

I bend down and start sponging the floor and the side of the counter.

"Oh, great," says Mom. "I really appreciate your bringing it over." He shrugs. I read his shirt: "I used to be schizophrenic, but we're okay now." "Why don't you stay for dessert, Brendan? I bought mango sorbet. We'd love to have you join us. I can't remember the last time you two played chess."

Brendan looks down at me. I look at the sponge and begin scrubbing again. "I guess I should be going," says Brendan.

So go, I want to shout.

"Just a minute," says Mom. "I have something for Beth."

The phone rings and my mother answers. "Oh,

hello, Antonia," she says. "How is everything going with the contest?"

I pop up and run over, wanting to grab the phone out of her hands. Antonia says something that makes my mother nod. "I'll put her on," says Mom. My mother isn't angry, so Antonia couldn't have told her that the plays are still in the car. I'm positive Antonia found them and has begun reading. Mom hands the phone to me and I take it.

"Hello," I say. Mom leaves the room. Brendan stares at me. I turn around because I can't concentrate with him looking at me.

"Sarah," says Antonia. "I'm having a gathering. Unfortunately my cohorts have found me. Would you pop over? Say in an hour? I could use your calming energy. Actually, you might find some of these people interesting. I used to." I smile. She's inviting me to hang out at her gathering. I like the idea of a gathering. It seems informal, spontaneous, yet filled with possibilities.

"Sure," I say. "I'll be there."

"Wonderful. Do you have my address? I'm staying in a lovely little bungalow."

"I know where you are." I hang up the phone and turn. Mom is back, carrying a large envelope, which she hands to Brendan.

"What's up?" she asks me.

I'm not about to tell her that Antonia is having a gathering. "Antonia needs help with the contest," I lie.

"Whatever for?" she asks.

I shrug. "I'm her assistant."

"You mean *now*?"

I nod.

"It's getting dark," says my mother. "You can't go over now."

"I have to. She needs me."

"Georgina is leaving, so I can't drive you and I won't let you go alone. Call her back and tell her that you'll help her tomorrow."

"But, Mom. Antonia is a spontaneous person. She needs to work now, when the mood strikes her."

"Tell her to strike the mood tomorrow." Mom leaves.

How can I tell Antonia I'm not coming to her gathering? She needs me because I have a calming effect on her. And I can hand her my finished play.

Brendan's still staring at me. "So what are you going to do?" he asks. "Tell Antonia you can't come, or do what I'd do—go anyway?"

"How can I go if Mom forbids it?"

"And I thought you were starting to show some spunk."

"I have plenty of spunk." I'm hurt when he looks at me like he doesn't believe me. "Didn't I stand up to your mother about not selling the raffles?" He just looks at me with a smirk on his face. I hate Brendan Callahan.

"If you're so spunky, then why are you doing an errand for your mother?"

"Because," he begins, then he changes his mind. "Oh, why did I bother? See ya around."

"See ya," I answer. When he leaves, I pick up the receiver and put it down again. If I don't go, I'll probably regret it the rest of my life. I pace around the kitchen. I finish putting the leftovers away. I pace some more and look at the clock. Brendan's right. If I want to be an amazing creative person, then I can't allow my mother to stifle me. I'm going to that gathering.

In the living room, Jason sleeps in my mother's arms. She puts her finger to her lips when she sees me and motions to the baby. Georgina waves and slips out the front door.

"I'm going upstairs to write," I whisper.

She nods. Next to her is a lot of paperwork. Probably stories she's editing for the paper. That will keep her busy.

I grab my play, which I've already put in a pretty purple envelope. I put it, my notebook, and a flashlight in my backpack.

I haven't climbed out of the house from my window since I was a kid. I ran away once, when my mother wouldn't let me go on a class trip to the zoo. "The animals are being mistreated," she said. If only she had stopped there. But Mom became obsessed and wrote an exposé about conditions at the zoo. The zoo closed down for six months. Mom got congratulations, but my classmates gave me the silent treatment.

Quietly and carefully, I make my way along the tree branch close to my window and shinny down the tree, trying not to make any noise. I know I can bike to South Beach and back in a half hour. I'll stay for an hour, and that should get me back at a decent time.

I drop to the ground and slink over to the garage. I use the back door and walk the bike to the side of the house. I check to see if my mother is looking out. She's not, so I walk my bike out of the yard and down the block.

When I think I am safely out of sight, I mount the bike and start riding down the dark street. I feel free and very excited. I'm going to a famous writer's gathering!

"Hey!" I almost fall off my bike. "It took you long enough," says Brendan, smiling.

I smile back, proud of myself.

"Let's get going," he says.

"You're coming with me?"

"I figure you need guidance," he says. "Since you're so new to spunkiness."

I pretend to protest, but I'm happy to have company because it is getting dark and South Beach might be deserted.

"Let's do it in ten," he says, speeding off.

"Suit yourself," I say. "But I'm planning on eight."

SIXTEEN

We would have made it to Antonia's in less than eight minutes if we had known exactly where she was staying. As it turns out, we got a little lost. Brendan insisted he could find it if I gave him a little time, but I was in a rush to get to the gathering, so I asked a jogger for directions. She pointed to a group of bungalows in a secluded area overlooking the beach, called Quiet Retreat. Number 18, where Antonia is staying, is the most secluded of all.

We leave our bikes and climb the steps, with only the moonlight to guide us. South Beach is deserted. I won't let Brendan know I am the least bit scared.

When we get to the top landing, I knock on the door and a woman answers. At first I think it's Antonia, but then I realize this woman has a similar face, except her hair is darker and she's thinner.

"Hi," she says. "You must be Sally."

"Sarah," I say. She steps back to let me in. "This is my friend Brendan."

The lady looks at Brendan and gives him a sexy

smile. Brendan totally blushes. She extends a hand to him. "I'm Charlene DeMarco."

"Nice to meet you," he says. As I walk inside, I wonder if she is Antonia's sister. The bungalow is dimly lit. Candles burn all over the large front room. Antonia sits grandly at the dining room table, talking with a man and a woman. She is wearing another breathtaking ensemble, of turquoise and white chiffon. A cat, probably Ophelia, whizzes by my feet in pursuit of a fly.

"Dear girl," Antonia says. "I'm so glad you've come."

"I hope you don't mind that I brought a friend," I say.

"He's cute," says Antonia. This makes Brendan blush more.

Antonia introduces us to Charlene, who is her cousin and her agent. A super-thin lady named Margo is an assistant at a Hollywood studio. The tall and stocky man next to her is Roland, a producer. People from Hollywood! It makes me wish I had practiced a new cool, sophisticated look.

"Hello," I say to them.

Roland and Margo both give me an annoyed glance as if they don't want me here, but Antonia smiles warmly. "Do sit down," she says.

I sit in an empty seat and motion for Brendan to sit next to me.

"Have something." Antonia points to an assortment of delicious-looking desserts. She nibbles on a cream puff.

"We really have to talk about the script tonight," demands Roland. "You've been avoiding the issue since I got here. I have a meeting in LA tomorrow afternoon. Can I see what you've written so far?" He snaps his fingers.

"Impossible," says Antonia. "If I show you the script before it's finished, then that would destroy the entire creative process." She looks at me. "Isn't that right, Sarah?"

I nod.

"Tell them how involved and busy I am with your precious little contest."

"Antonia is very busy," I say to Roland. "She's judging our teen writing contest and there are *twenty-three* plays for her to read. She is our inspiration."

Margo rolls her eyes and the producer shakes his head. "At least give us an outline," says Margo. "Carl has to begin scouting locations."

"I can't presently divulge any information," says Antonia.

"And why not?" asks Roland. "Last month, you said you were almost finished."

"And the month before that," says Margo.

"The creative process cannot be put on a time schedule," says Antonia. "The muse works in strange ways. Only those blessed with the gift could possibly understand the process." She looks directly at me. Is it because she thinks I'm also blessed with the gift?

"I'm really getting agitated," says Roland, tossing back his head. "You promised me a great love story. I spoke to Bronson today. He's considering starring in it, but he wants details."

"Just let us take a peek at the script," says Margo, coaxingly.

"Impossible," says Antonia, giving me a pleading look.

"Um," I say. "As Antonia's personal assistant, I need her to put all her energy into the contest."

Roland huffs and struts over to Charlene. "Can't you do something to push this along? You're her agent."

"I've done my best. This is very hard on me, too." Charlene huffs and, with a quick turn, leaves the room. A moment of chilled silence follows, broken only by Ophelia bumping into the coffee table, still pursuing the fly. Roland paces around the room, mumbling about deadlines, disrespectful writers, and contracts. A cell phone rings and Margo whips one out of her purse and takes the call. Antonia rubs her temples.

Brendan leans in to me. "This is one dead party."

"That's because it's a gathering," I whisper.

"Hey," he says out loud. "Why did the turtle cross the road? To get to the Shell station!"

No one, besides Brendan, laughs.

"How about this one," he says. "Did you hear about the shoe factory that burned down? Two hundred soles were lost." When no one laughs this time, Brendan slaps the table. "Now I know that's funny."

"Have a piece of cake," says Antonia.

"I don't want a piece of cake," he says. "I'm a comedian and you're supposed to laugh."

"I understand." She hands him a cookie. He takes it.

Margo waves to Roland. "Bronson wants to talk to you."

"What am I supposed to tell him?"

Margo cups her hand over the receiver. "Ask him for a little patience," she whispers. Roland grabs the phone and walks into the living room with it. He talks softly so I can't make out what he's saying, but I wonder if he's talking to Bronson McGee, the top-box office movie star? I loved him in *The Sinking of the Andrea Doria.*

Antonia smiles at me as she nervously plays with an earring.

Roland walks back, his phone call over. He leans over Antonia. "I'll give you one more week, and then I want to see the script. Remember, you signed a contract. If you don't produce a script, this will end up in court."

"I'll have it in a week," says Antonia.

"Margo," says Roland, snapping his fingers. "Let's move. We can still catch the red-eye to LA."

"I'm right behind you," she says.

As they gather their things, Antonia smiles and waves to them. "Ta, ta," she says. "Talk to you in a week."

I follow Roland to the door. "I was just curious," I say. "Was that *the* Bronson McGee you were talking to?"

"Is there another?" he says in a sarcastic tone.

"Ask him what kind of coffee they served on the *Andrea Doria*," says Brendan. "Sanka." He laughs.

"Shhhh," I tell him. Margo and Roland leave. Antonia sighs and leans back in her chair.

"This is the worst audience I've ever met," says Brendan. "Or was it me?" Brendan bites his lip.

"You're fine," I say. Antonia looks even sadder than Brendan. "Is there anything I can do to help?" I move closer. I'm curious if she has worked on the script at all. Maybe I could help her finish it. I'd probably have to go to Hollywood with her. We could rent a bungalow in Malibu. We'd entertain Bronson McGee. This could be the beginning of my screenwriting career. Provided, of course, that my mother would let me go.

Antonia drops her head. "I don't feel well. This has been a most unpleasant evening."

"You can say that again," says Brendan.

"Shhh," I say. "Would you like to lie down?"

She nods.

"Take my arm." I walk with her to the bedroom down the hall.

"I can't believe they found me here in Staten Island, of all places," she says. "I suppose I should leave, but where would I go?"

"You can't leave," I say. "You have to judge the contest. And you will finish that screenplay because I will help you. I'm a very good writer. I have dozens of notebooks filled with ideas. I'll show you all of them. We'll work day and night and we'll finish it by next week."

"That will be marvelous." She pats my arm. We get to the bed and she lies down. Her cousin is sitting in a chair, looking out the window.

"I'll be right back," I say. I run into the other room and take my play out of my backpack and run back into the bedroom. "I have a final play to give you. Can I put it with the rest?"

"Whatever." She waves her hand. I look around, trying to find the plays, but I don't see them.

"Remember that folder I gave you earlier, Antonia? Where is it?"

"Which folder?"

"The folder with the plays. The plays you are supposed to read for the contest."

"Oh," she says, fluffing a pillow. "I'm not sure where that is."

"I put it in the backseat of your car."

She yawns.

"Do you think they are still in the car?" I ask.

"It's very possible." She curls up on the bed and rests her head on the pillow. Ophelia meows and walks across Antonia's body, trying to find a comfortable spot. She rubs the side of her face against Antonia and already I can hear snoring.

"I have to find those plays," I tell Brendan.

"Where's your car?" he asks, shaking Antonia's shoulder.

"Oh, that thing. I returned it earlier this evening." She turns over, almost knocking Ophelia over.

"Brendan, they have to be around here. Help me find them." I turn to Charlene. "Do you know where the plays are?"

She shakes her head. "No idea."

We search everywhere, even the bathroom. No folder. No plays.

"What am I going to do?" I am almost at the point of hysteria. I'm responsible for them. My mother will kill me. She'll kill Antonia. The only good part of this is that Anne Marie's play is among the missing.

"Which rental company did you use?" Brendan asks Antonia. All we hear is snoring.

We ask Charlene. "No idea," she says, rising. "I'm leaving."

"But you have to help us find the plays. You're her agent."

She laughs. "Whoop-dee-doo. She hasn't written

anything publishable in years. Who do you think wrote *Enraptured Thorns in My Heart*?"

"What do you mean?" I ask.

"I wrote the book as a favor to Aunt Edna. It's not hard to copy Antonia's style, except I improved upon it. Don't you agree?"

"I loved it. It's Antonia's best. . . . I mean, uh . . ." She smiles. I sit on the bed because my mind feels fuzzy. The fact that Antonia didn't write my favorite book does not want to settle in my brain.

"I owe Aunt Edna a lot. She raised me when my mother and father died. Poor Auntie, she's under the delusion that her daughter is going through a temporary writer's block. Only I don't think it's temporary. It's high time I moved on to write under my own name."

"Well, sure," I say, but I'm thinking about Antonia and how she told that interviewer at the bookstore that she's an orphan. "Who's Aunt Edna?" I ask.

"Antonia's mother."

I look over at Antonia. "But—"

"Is she still telling people she's an orphan? It drives poor Aunt Edna nuts." Charlene walks over to me and pats my shoulder. "Take my advice and find yourself another judge."

She walks into the other room. I follow this woman who wrote my favorite book. She picks up a bag and leaves, slamming the door behind her.

I stare at the door. Antonia didn't write *Enraptured Thorns in My Heart*! I can't believe this. And she doesn't seem to care at all about Mom's plays. *She's supposed to care deeply about things.*

"It's getting late," says Brendan. "We'd better go."

"I have to find those plays!" I'm almost screaming.

He shakes his head. "We'll look tomorrow. Right now, we need to go home."

I look at my watch. It's 10:40. How did it get this late? I run back into the bedroom. "I'll call you first thing tomorrow," I say, even though I know she can't hear me. I want to shake her—not just awake, but into the Antonia she's supposed to be.

"Come on!" yells Brendan. I throw my play in my backpack. We run down the stairs to our bikes.

Brendan rides with me to my house. He follows as I walk the bike along the side of the house and put it in the garage. "See you tomorrow," he says. Just then the backdoor light comes on.

"Where have you been?" screams my mother.

SEVENTEEN

"How could you sneak out of the house without telling me?" Mom is simultaneously scolding me and telling the police that I've been found.

I look down at the floor. "We just felt like going out for a ride," says Brendan.

"Until 11:00 at night?" she asks.

I look at Brendan.

"It's good exercise," he says.

"You're always saying that I should go riding with Brendan," I chime in.

"During the day is what I meant," says Mom. She pulls at her hair. "Where were you?" I hold my breath. If she is this mad because I stayed out late, I don't want to be around for the explosion when she finds out the plays are missing.

"We were just riding around," says Brendan.

"You weren't visiting that DeMarco woman, were you?" says my mother, her eyes narrowing.

"Who's she?" asks Brendan.

"It has nothing to do with her," I say.

"I'm going to have a word with her, just to make sure."

My heart sinks. What if I can't find the plays before she talks with Antonia? Why is this happening? I trusted Antonia.

"You can't leave without letting me know where you are going. You scared me. You could have gotten hurt."

"But we didn't, Mrs. Simmons."

"That's not the point. Parents make rules for a reason. I'm very surprised by your behavior tonight. I thought I could trust you to act sensibly. You're grounded for two weeks."

"But—"

"Not another word or I'll make it longer. I'm going to have to tell your father about this."

Mom picks up her cell and dials. "Beth, they're here. Come and get Brendan."

"I don't need her to come and get me," says Brendan.

"Well, I do." She dials another number.

"Who are you calling now?" I ask.

"Antonia DeMarco. I have a feeling all this has something to do with her."

I cross my fingers, hoping Antonia won't pick up.

"Hmmm, no answer," says Mom. She hangs up and I sigh with relief. "I'll visit her tomorrow." Mom turns to me. "If I find out that woman has had anything to do with the two of you going out tonight, I'll have her arrested, and I mean that."

I get up, not knowing what else to do.

"You'll leave your bike in our garage, Brendan," says Mom. "You can pick it up tomorrow."

"I only live three blocks away," says Brendan.

"Tomorrow," she repeats.

I walk Brendan into the foyer. "Thanks for not saying anything," I whisper. "I don't want Mom to know that she's right about Antonia."

"I hear ya, but you'd better call that wacko and make her find those plays," he whispers.

Outside, a car pulls up.

"Good night," Brendan says to me. "Good night, Mrs. Simmons." My mother doesn't say a word as Brendan disappears into the night.

I turn back to face my mother.

"I thought better of Brendan. I really did," she mumbles.

I smooth out some of the newly formed spikes in her hair, sorry to have caused them. She punches numbers into the phone.

"Who are you calling?"

"Your father. He should be up by now."

I slip out and walk upstairs. I can't bear to be scolded twice in one night. I close the door and plop into my window seat. I put my head between my knees. Where are the plays? What will happen if I don't find them?

• • •

In the morning, Mom greets Georgina with last night's story. "She's not to leave the house under any circumstances," says my mother. "She's grounded for two weeks." Georgina promises to call Mom if I give her any trouble. Great. Now Georgina is my babysitter.

"What time are you planning to visit Antonia?" I ask.

"This afternoon," she says.

Mom leaves for work, but not before reminding me, once again—just in case I forgot—that I'm grounded.

As soon as Mom leaves, Georgina says, "It looks like you're in big trouble."

I'm so angry. "Go ahead, enjoy my misery," I tell her. "At least I'm not a phony like you. If my mother knew how you roll up her expensive carpet and dance around her priceless antiques, she'd ground you, too!" I storm into the kitchen.

I dial Antonia's number. I let it ring thirty times, but she doesn't pick up. I pace around the kitchen. I have to find Antonia. I have to find the plays, but how can I do that if I'm grounded?

Georgina breezes into the kitchen. "Go away," I say.

"Can I speak to you for a moment?"

"No." I go upstairs, plop down into my window seat, and stare. Georgina knocks at the door. "Are you checking up on me?"

"No. I want to speak to you."

"I already told you, I don't want to talk."

Georgina walks in anyway and sits down beside me and I breathe in her gentle rose scent. "I can see why you like sitting here. It's a good place for dreaming. I used to have a special place when I was little. I liked to climb to the roof of our house. It made me feel like I was queen of the world."

I fold my arms.

"I'm sorry that you're grounded."

I shrug.

"So, you've seen me dancing?"

"You haven't come up here to be nice. You want to make sure I don't tell my mother."

"That's not true. I'm glad you know I'm a dancer. It's what I am."

"So why did you lie to my mother?"

"I get impressions from people. And something about her told me she might not hire a dancer to look after her son."

"You mean she's closed-minded," I say.

"A bit," says Georgina. "But it's not an uncommon reaction."

"Why aren't you dancing?" I have to know. "You're the best dancer I've ever seen."

"It's complicated, Sarah. I would be dancing, but I have responsibilities."

"Like what?"

She stares out the window. "I popped over to America to look after Granddad. He's a stubborn old thing with a big heart problem. He likes to think he can take care of himself, but he can't even remember to take his medicines. How can I leave him, when there's no one else to look after him?"

"But you're so talented," I say. "Can't you find someone else to help him?"

She turns back to me. "Tried that, but Granddad ran away. I'm the only person he trusts."

"But you have to dance."

"I do, in private. The piece you saw me dancing is for an audition. A mate told me about a small company that will be touring Europe in the fall."

"That's great."

"Granddad will go nutter when he finds out."

"You have to make him understand," I say.

Georgina shakes her head. "Easier said than done. I'm considering a nursing home, but it will break his heart, and mine. Meanwhile, I practice secretly, except, of course, when people like you spy on me."

"It's not fair," I say. "Your granddad needs to see how talented you are. It's like you and the dance are one. You're incredible. I want to be that good at something."

"How about that play you're writing?" She winks. "That's good."

I pick up a pillow and squeeze it to my chest. "How do you know about it? I haven't shown it to anyone."

She scrunches her nose. "Sorry," she says, "I was curious about you, too. I took a little peek one day, and I ended up reading the whole way through."

"You read it? You shouldn't have done that!"

"Sorry, but I was curious about what you were doing cooped up in your room all day."

"Did you like it?"

"I did."

"Really?"

"Really."

"It's for the contest. Do you think I have a shot at winning?"

"Very possibly, Victoria. You have a definite sense of the dramatic."

"If there is a contest." I tell her everything that happened last night. It's a relief to tell someone. "I have to find the plays, but I can't do that because I'm grounded."

"Hmmm." She thinks. "If I were you, I'd call the car rental companies straightaway."

"But I'll eventually have to go get them."

"Well," she says, "I promised your mum that I wouldn't let you leave the house, but I can't watch you all the time. I mean, if you were to leave when I was busy doing something else, then how would I know?"

"You wouldn't tell on me?" I ask.

"Just don't tell me, okay?"

"Thank you," I say, knowing I don't exactly deserve this favor. Up to now, I haven't been that nice to her.

She gets up and walks toward the door.

"Georgina," I call. "Would you still like to borrow my hat?"

She smiles. "That would be lovely."

Georgina looks and acts so confident, but underneath, she's struggling to do what she wants, just like me. That's really, truly, deeply amazing. And Antonia. I've sat right here, adoring her, thinking she was this creative, lovable person, but she's really, truly, deeply a liar. Until yesterday, I considered myself a good judge of character. I thought that would make me a great writer. Now, I truly, deeply don't know what to think.

EIGHTEEN

In the phone book, I find listings for five car rental companies. I call, explaining that I left important papers in the backseat of a convertible. I get through to four of the five companies. None of them found a package of plays. When I dial the fifth company, Rent-a-Dream, an answering machine comes on and I leave my phone number.

I go back to my room and wait for them to call back. A pebble hits my window. Brendan leans against his bike in the middle of the backyard. Today's shirt reads, "Yes, I'm spoiled, so what's your point?"

"Hey!" he yells. "What's happening?"

"I'm grounded. Aren't you?"

"No."

That is so unfair!

"Want to take a ride to Antonia's?"

"I'm grounded," I repeat.

"On a spunkiness scale of one to ten, that would be a negative two," he says, grinning. "But then, spunkiness needs constant practice."

"I'm in enough trouble. Besides, I have to wait to hear back from a car rental company."

"Too bad," he says. "But, of course, if you'd rather sit inside and watch the rest of us carrying on with our lives . . ."

Why is he so irritating? Why does he always seem to make sense? I hope I'm not going to regret this, but I crawl out the window and hop onto the branch. The climb down is easier because I don't have to be quiet.

"Is that Sarah?" He leans back, crossing his arms, like he's appraising me. "The girl who's *grounded*?"

I stare at him. "You love it when I break the rules, don't you?"

"Yeah, I do." Our eyes lock. "It's a total ten." I blush. He leans in and kisses me. It's a *wow*!

"You'd better stop kissing me," he says.

"I wasn't kissing you," I protest. "You were kissing me."

"That's ridiculous," he says. "And you'll never prove it."

What nerve! I'm never going to let him kiss me again. I don't care how good a kisser he is. I get my bike out of the garage and we ride to South Beach.

I pedal fast and hard, filled with so many different feelings. Fear that someone might see me and tell my mother. Determination to find Antonia before my mother does. Total shock that I am once again defying my mother. And then there's the fact that Brendan is here. I'm not sure what emotion that is.

I spot a Volvo coming in our direction and turn off the main street. It probably isn't my mother, but I'm not taking any chances.

We pass a parked ice-cream truck and Brendan says, "How do astronauts eat their ice cream?" I shrug. "In floats."

I laugh, but I'm trying to concentrate on what to say to Antonia. In a matter of minutes, we'll be at her bungalow. I must be strong. She must help me.

"Did you hear about the ice-cream man that was found dead in his van? He was lying on the floor covered in nuts and raspberry sauce. The police believe he topped himself." He taps my shoulder. "You don't think my jokes are funny, do you?"

"Sure, they're funny."

"Last night, no one laughed, and they're in the entertainment business. I'm worried."

"They were a little preoccupied."

He shakes his head. "I'm going to bomb at the Java Café."

"You'll be fine," I say.

"You really think so?"

I nod. We reach the boardwalk and I feel better as I inhale the ocean air. Antonia *will* help me.

At the top of the steps, a man is pounding on

Antonia's door. "Open up. You won't get away with this!" he yells. "There are laws on my side."

Brendan motions for me to stay behind as he approaches the man. "Can I help you, sir?"

"I need to find Antonia DeMarco."

"You've come to the right place," says Brendan. "I guess she's out."

"Where is she?" The man turns. He's large, with a mean and angry face. He's wearing dark blue overalls and his hair is uncombed and sticking up in the back. Is he some kind of crazy person?

"Maybe we should leave," I whisper to Brendan.

"We don't know where she is," Brendan says. "We'll stay and wait."

"I'll wait too," says the man. "She returned my new and expensive convertible with a big dent in the fender."

"That's terrible," I say, moving closer. "So, you're from the rental car company?"

"Rent-a-Dream," he says. "Right now, it's rent with a dent."

"That's funny," says Brendan. The man glares. "I didn't mean the situation, just the rhyme."

"That's terrible. It was such a nice car," I say.

"What do you know about the dent?"

"Nothing," I answer. "It's just that Ms. DeMarco left something in the car that belongs to my mother."

"What did she leave?" he asks.

"A folder full of plays for a contest. My mother doesn't know they're missing yet, and she'll kill me if I don't get them back. So do you think you could let me have them?" I tilt my head, hoping to look cool and respectable.

He smiles. "Sure. You can have what's inside."

"Oh, thank you, thank you." I can't believe it. I have the plays back. My mother will never know any of this happened. I've never been happier—

"All you have to do is pay for the dent; then you can take whatever you want." He leans against the side of the house.

I look at Brendan. "How much would it cost?" he asks.

"Fifteen-fifty," the man says coldly.

"Fifteen dollars and fifty cents? I have that at ho—"

"Fifteen hundred and fifty dollars!"

Brendan whistles. "That's a lot of money."

"I know." The man looks at me. "This woman has acted irresponsibly with my property. Has she sent you here to bargain with me? Is that woman your mother?"

"No, she's not."

He shrugs. "Whatever. When I called her, she insisted I made the dent. She refuses to pay."

"Sue her," says Brendan.

"Or charge her credit card," I add.

He shakes his head. "That crazy lady said she'll dispute the charges. She said no one will believe me. I am a small businessman who doesn't want any trouble. I have three kids and a wife to feed. I can't wait while I have to fight with her credit company. It will take months to straighten out. If I can't rent that car, I could go out of business."

"Antonia took advantage of both of us," I say.

"She's a bad lady," he says.

"Could we compromise?" says Brendan. "Since you're both in trouble."

"Like what?" asks the man.

"We'll talk her into paying you, and you can give the plays to Sarah."

"It isn't fair to the people who wrote those plays," I say. "They have nothing to do with this. A lot of innocent kids are going to suffer."

"I can't let you have them until I get a guarantee that the dent will be paid for. I'm sorry." He looks at his watch. "I have to get back to work. Tell that crazy woman I'll be back."

We watch him leave.

"What am I going to do?" I say.

I hear a noise below. We peer over the railing. Antonia is quietly sneaking up the stairs. She reaches the landing, looking in the direction of the man. She turns to go in the bungalow but stops when she sees me. She's wearing big sunglasses and a beautiful purple and pink sundress, and she's carrying an expensive-looking tote bag. She still looks like a movie star. I want to run up and fling my arms around her. Instead, I say, "Antonia, you have to pay that man."

She turns and bolts down the stairs.

NINETEEN

e race after her.

"Antonia!"

"Not now," she says. "Go away, Sally."

"It's Sarah!" She quickens her pace.

"Stop," I say, grabbing her arm.

"I really have to go." She tries to pull away. "No! Please!" She frees her arm.

"Antonia, you have to pay for that dent."

"Sarah's plays are in that car," adds Brendan. "The man won't give them back until you pay."

Antonia fans herself. "It's so hot. I can't think. I need to sit down. I need water."

"Let's go back upstairs," I suggest.

"No." She backs away. "I can't go back there. He'll find me."

"Just pay him and get it over with," says Brendan. "Fifteen-fifty isn't that much for a best-selling author."

"It's not Mr. Rent-a-Dream I'm worried about." She sobs. "You don't know the trouble I'm in." She sways and I grab her. "Please, get me something to drink. I'm dizzy."

"Come upstairs, I'll find something."

"No, I can't. . . . Please . . . Water . . . My blood pressure . . . I'll pass out."

"Brendan, do you mind? I'll stay with her."

"Better you than me." He walks toward the boardwalk.

Antonia stumbles, weaving among the sunbathers. She reaches the water's edge, kneels, and fans herself with her hat. She looks like a child who's lost her parents.

I sit in the wet sand next to her. A little girl runs by, giggling as she tries to escape a wave. "Oh, to be young again," says Antonia. "To start over so my life wouldn't be in ruins."

"It's not in ruins," I say. "You have a lot of fans and a movie deal."

"I'm in big trouble, child. Charlene wrote *Enraptured Thorns in My Heart.* She gets all the royalties. I pay alimony to three husbands who've never worked a day in their lives. They're young, handsome, and blood-thirsty." She scoops a fistful of sand and lets it slowly seep out of her hand. "I have dozens of credit cards. Every one of them is maxed out. There are collection agencies who would like to find me, too. And then there's this annoying little man who says I stole his plot for *Love Hath No Fury.*"

"Did you?" I ask.

"It's possible that I might have read his manuscript at a writer's conference. I really don't remember. He can't sue me. I'm broke. So he called me this morning and said he is going to go to the press."

"You don't even have the fifteen hundred and fifty dollars."

She shakes her head. Brendan returns with a bottle of water. Antonia gulps it down.

We watch the waves for a while. "Antonia's broke."

"But she's a best-selling author."

"She has tons of financial problems. I kind of feel sorry for her."

"Well, I don't." He turns to Antonia. "You can't be broke. You have to pay for that dent. Not to mention the two bucks you owe me for the water."

She sniffles. "No one understands me, not even you, Sally. You're just like all the others."

"My name is Sarah! And I'm not like the others! I trusted you and you let me down! You have to find a way to pay for that dent! I need those plays!"

"I have to pack, find Ophelia, and get away from here before that nasty man comes with the press."

"But what about all those young writers who are counting on you to judge this contest? And there's my mother. She'll be furious."

She gets up and heads toward the boardwalk, moving swiftly for a person who was dizzy just a few minutes ago.

We follow her. "I'll make her stay, if I have to sit on her," I say to Brendan.

He smiles. "On the spunkiness scale, that's an eight."

"Only eight!" We start up the steep stairs after her. Upstairs, someone is knocking loudly.

"Ms. DeMarco! Are you in there?"

We freeze. "It's my mother!" I whisper.

"This way," says Brendan. "Before she sees us."

Like in a fire drill, the three of us move quickly and quietly, scurrying under the boardwalk.

"Antonia DeMarco! Open the door!" calls my mother. Antonia winces.

We hear footsteps above our heads. *Don't come down here! Please, Mom.* As if reading my mind, Brendan grabs my hand and squeezes it. I can't breathe. After a bit, she stomps down the stairs and I pray that she doesn't come out on the beach. Finally, her footsteps retreat and she's gone. I breathe.

As we crawl out from under the boardwalk, a woman with a great tan and a bright orange bathing suit walks by. She glances our way and stops. "Are you Antonia DeMarco? I just love *Enraptured Thorns in My Heart.* How did you come up with the idea?"

Now I understand why she doesn't like that question.

Antonia looks at her for a long moment, wet sand clinging to her wrinkled sundress. "No, I'm not

Antonia DeMarco. People mistake me for her all the time. I'm nobody."

We go to a diner a block up from the beach. It's lunchtime, so it's crowded with workers from a nearby hospital.

"I can't stand being such a failure," says Antonia.

We go to a booth toward the back. Brendan and I sit facing Antonia. When the waitress comes by, Antonia orders a Waldorf salad and a double espresso.

"Who's going to pay for all this food?" whispers Brendan.

I don't know what to say.

Brendan turns to a group of nurses sitting at a booth across from us. "Hey," he says. "Did you hear about the woman who walked into the emergency room? She says, 'Doctor, Doctor, my little boy just swallowed a roll of film!' 'Hmmm,' says the doctor. 'Let's hope nothing develops.'"

The nurses laugh. "Finally, a good audience," he says.

He gets up and leans against the edge of their booth. "Another woman runs into the hospital, saying, 'Doctor, Doctor, my son swallowed my pen, what should I do?' The doctor says, 'Use a pencil till I get there.'"

"Hey, this kid is funny," one says. "We can sure use someone like you in the emergency room. Stop in sometime, we all work there."

Brendan continues. "Two doctors . . ."

I'm happy for him. I stare into my glass of water. So far this week, I've been wrong about Georgina, Brendan, and Antonia. Not a good average. I hate admitting that Mom is a better judge of character than I am. Maybe it's me who's closed-minded.

Antonia moves the lettuce around on her plate. Then she puts down the fork and looks deep into my eyes. "If only I could turn my life around."

"You can," I say. "Start small by finding the money to pay for the dent. Think of all the young writers you'll be helping."

She nods. "You're very wise and very right."

"You must have money somewhere."

She shakes her head.

"Couldn't you sell something, like a piece of jewelry?"

She wipes her mouth. "Maybe. It's just that I can't think straight with all those people after me. If only I had someplace safe to go, just for a day or two. So I could calm down." She smiles shyly. "Could you find such a place for me?" She puts her hand over mine. "You're the only person who's been nice to me. Help me begin to redeem myself. All I need is a little time." Her eyes look teary and I hand her another napkin.

"Okay, I'll try, but don't just *say* you want to help me. You have to swear that you'll really help me."

"Absolutely. With your help, I will turn my life around."

Can I trust her? Do I have a choice? Where can I hide her? Where, where, where? I rack my brain, but only one place comes to mind.

There's a public phone in the lobby. I dial. It rings several times. She picks up.

"It's me," I say.

"It can't be Sarah," says Georgina. "I just told Sarah's mother that Sarah is upstairs where *Sarah* is supposed to be."

"This is Vicky," I say. "I need a really big favor."

"What is it, *Vicky*?"

"Antonia is in a lot of financial trouble. Can you take her home with you? Just for one night. It'll give her some extra time to come up with the money. When we get the plays back, I'll sit with her until she reads them."

"No way," answers Georgina.

"Please. It will only be for one night. I can't take her to my house or to Brendan's. I don't know what else to do."

There's silence on the other end. "Georgina?" My voice cracks.

After a long moment, she sighs. "For some strange reason, Granddad loves her books."

"Then you'll do it?"

"Yes. But you really owe me now. Where are you?"

"We're at the Dolphin Diner on Sand Lane. Can you come and get her?"

"I can't come for Antonia unless Sarah is here to take care of the baby."

"Sarah will be right there."

"Good. She should hurry because her mum's on her way home."

"One other thing. Could you bring enough money for a Waldorf salad and a double espresso?" I hang up and go back to the booth. "Antonia, I found somewhere for you to stay tonight."

"Where?" asks Brendan.

"With Georgina."

"The dancer?"

"Yes." I turn to Antonia. "You'll be safe there, but you have to promise me that you will find something to sell."

She pats my arm. "Absolutely."

"Brendan, I have to get home. Will you stay with Antonia until Georgina picks her up?"

"I'm supposed to meet someone. It's important."

"Could you postpone it for an hour? This is very important. We shouldn't leave her alone."

He looks through his pockets. "I'll see if I have her number."

Her number? Is it Anne Marie Valgetti?

TWENTY

I get home minutes before Mom. Breathe. Pretend everything's normal. I grab one of Jason's storybooks and read to him about a naughty mouse. Mom walks into the living room and smiles. "Having fun?"

"You bet," I say. "Right, Jason?" It's a good thing he can't talk yet.

She pulls at her hair. "I stopped by Antonia's, but she wasn't there. Do you know where she is?"

"No idea," I say.

Mom kisses us both. "Has Georgina left?"

"She had to do something important."

Mom stretches. "I'd like to feel human again. Do you mind if I take a short soak to wash away a rotten day?"

"Take your time."

"Thank you, honey." Mom goes upstairs. A little while later, I take Jason into the kitchen and dial Georgina.

"Granddad is thrilled to meet Antonia. He put on his tux, which he hasn't worn since 1952."

"Has she thought of something to sell yet?"

"All she's done so far is talk, talk, talk about her problems. She's annoying."

"Sorry," I say. "Remind her that she has to find something worth fifteen-fifty."

"Will do."

"And tomorrow morning," I say, "we have to make a plan so she's never alone."

"Don't worry," she says. "Granddad will keep an eye on her. When he gets attached, it's not easy to get away."

I hang up. Jason wriggles in my arms. "Please be good," I say, wishing he could understand. "I'm in the middle of a crisis." I rock him and he settles down a little. I really appreciate Georgina's help, but I'm having major doubts believing Antonia is going to help me.

Mom, dressed in a long, silky robe, enters the kitchen. Her hair is wet but neat again. "Is something wrong?" she asks.

"No."

"Then can I have my cutie?" I hand Jason to Mom. He gurgles.

I go to my room and pace. I take out my notebook and cross out every nice thing I wrote about Antonia. In its place, I write *selfish, annoying, misguided,* and *totally clueless.* I thumb back through the book. These are the same words I've used to describe my mother. I throw the notebook under the bed.

Later, there's a knock on my door. "Hey," says

Mom. "How about grilled chicken for dinner?" I'm in the window seat, facing out, so she can't see I'm crying.

"Sure."

She moves to the window seat and turns my head around. "What's wrong?"

"Nothing."

"You're sitting here crying about nothing?" I nod. She sits. "Has Brendan done something to upset you?"

"No," I say.

Mom puts her arm around my shoulder. "I hate to admit this, but maybe I've been wrong about him. Maybe under that nice exterior is wildness. If he has made you do anything against your will, you can tell me."

I stare at her in disbelief. Is my mother alluding to sex? "Mom," I say. "Brendan and I haven't done anything."

Relief washes over her face. She kisses my forehead. "You shut me out a lot, you know. Your father says it's all part of growing up. But I don't like it, all the same."

I nod.

"That offer to look for another writing contest is still open, if you're interested," she says.

I don't say anything, and then we just sit there in silence for what seems an eternity. Finally, she slips out of the room. Once she's gone, I start crying because it would have been a relief to tell her everything. I remember a time when I could.

After dinner, I go to bed, burying my face in the pillow. I sleep lightly, waking again and again from unpleasant dreams.

"Sarah!" I open my eyes. Georgina stares down at me. It must be morning because the sun is up. "I've got bad news."

I bolt up. "What's wrong?"

"Antonia is gone!"

"How can she be gone?" I yell. "You were supposed to watch her."

"Shhh. Your mum will hear."

I lower my voice. "Tell me what happened."

She sits on the bed. "When I got up, she had already left. Granddad said Antonia called a cab an hour ago. He tried to convince her to stay, but Antonia was in a very excitable mood. She muttered something about leaving for Fiji and how they wouldn't be able to find her there."

"Fiji! You can't go there if you're broke."

"Your friend drove me crazy. She talked constantly about how her life was in ruins. This went on all night. I couldn't stand it, so I went into the backyard and danced. It's the only way I can relax. So, I am really tired today and it's probably why I didn't hear her leave"

"She lied to me again." I rock on the bed, stunned. "If she can afford to go to Fiji, then she could have paid to get my plays back. She's a horrible person. What am I going to do now?"

"I'm so sorry, Sarah."

Mom pops her head in. She's already dressed for work. "Anything wrong?"

"No, Mom."

"Be down in a minute," says Georgina.

Mom leaves.

"What am I going to tell my mother?"

Georgina takes an envelope out of her pocket. "I think this is for you." She hands it to me. The envelope is addressed to "Sally." The least Antonia could have done was get my name right. I tear open the envelope and take out the note.

Dear Sally,

I'm overcome with creativity!!! I feel rejuvenated and inspired after not being able to write for three years!! I'm off to Fiji to begin the screenplay. Sorry I couldn't say good-bye in person, but I need to track down an old friend who works for Worldwide Airlines.

Last night I watched in total rapture as a divine nymphet danced in the moonlight. She moved with passion and total abandon. She was bewitching. I knew instantly that the movie should be about her. This nymphet is filled with heavenly abilities, but is trapped in a mundane and weary existence, toiling each day as a nanny and having to come home to deal with an exploitive and interfering relative. Dancing alone under the stars is her only escape. Oh,

Sally. My torturous block has ended. I will redeem myself.
What life offers you, and when it offers, take it all!
Yours, Antonia

I stare at the letter. Georgina grabs it and reads. "Imagine me, the star of a movie."

"Don't gloat. I'm in a lot of trouble."

"Sorry. Really it's a terrible situation." She stares at the letter. "Divine nymphet. Brilliant. Did you say Bronson McGee might play my love interest?"

I give her a look.

"Sorry," she says. "It's just overwhelming to be the inspiration for a movie and to have such a boyfriend." I pluck the letter away from her. Not only has Antonia left me in the worst possible situation with my mom, but you would think, after all she put me through, that the least she could have done was made me the star of her screenplay. I was willing to help her write it.

"What are you going to do about the contest?" asks Georgina.

"Oh, I don't know," I say. "Let's see. I'll rob a bank. You can be my accomplice, but I'm sure you can dance your way out of getting arrested."

"I sense that you're mad at me, Sarah."

I shrug. "It's not your fault," I mumble.

"You're so right it isn't. I did you a favor, remember?"

I shrug again. "Going to prison will be a lot easier than telling my mother the plays are gone."

"Sarah," says Georgina. "Tell your mother the truth now, before this gets any messier."

I know Georgina is right. I follow her downstairs, thinking about how I'm going to tell Mom the truth. *Mom. Pass the orange juice and, by the way, the plays are missing.*

Mom is in the kitchen being Mom. She has Jason nestled in the crook of her arm as he drinks his bottle. Her other hand is holding her cell phone to her ear. She's talking to Joe about today's feature headline— something about a three-car collision on the express-way. "If Sam can't cover it," she says, "I'll stop there on the way in." Even though she's the managing editor, she never minds filling in for a reporter. I don't know why I'm thinking about this. I should be preparing myself for doom, but I want to savor this moment when my mother still doesn't know I'm a complete failure.

Georgina takes the baby from Mom and continues to feed him.

"Oh, no. What time is the meeting?" Mom begins throwing papers into her briefcase. "No, tell Maria, we can't take a position on this without looking at all the facts. I want background material on my desk in an hour. Hold on a sec." She turns to Georgina. "I have to go. I'll call you later."

"Um, Mom," I say. "I need to talk to you."

"Gotta run, honey. We'll talk tonight." She picks up her briefcase and goes back to talking on the cell phone. She passes me, turns back, and gives me a peck on the cheek.

"Joe, don't tell me Maria can't find background. She's got to find something. We can't do the story without it." She leaves the kitchen and walks toward the foyer. I follow. There couldn't be a worse time in the history of the world to tell my mother something like this. She's at the door.

"Mom," I yell.

She turns. "What, Sarah?"

When she looks at me, my throat tightens to the size of an atom. "Have a nice day," I croak with the last bit of air in my lungs.

"Um, all right," she says and heads out, still talking into her cell phone.

I go back into the living room and collapse onto the sofa. What if I never find the courage to tell her?

TWENTY-ONE

"You want me to tell her at work?"

"Look at it this way," Georgina says. "If you tell your mum at work, she won't be able to yell as much."

"But I can't."

Georgina pushes me toward the front door. "You've been driving me crazy since she left. Go and get this over with." She pushes me through the door. I protest, but I walk in the direction of Mom's office. The closer I get, the dumber Georgina's idea sounds. Mom can yell anywhere. I go inside anyway. The newsroom, as usual, is packed and noisy.

I wave at Joe. "Your mom's in a meeting."

"I'll wait in her office." I'm glad for the brief delay.

"Call me if you need anything."

I walk past Filipe Santo's desk, but he's on the phone. He switches the phone to his other ear and winks at me. He's shaved his moustache. He looked better with it.

Anne Marie isn't in the room, which is nice. I walk to Mom's office. The L-shaped desk with her computer on it faces the window. The section without the computer is piled with papers and folders. I look at the photos she has put along the back of the desk. There is one of her and Dad taken at a barbecue last summer and a few stupid school photos of me in different grades. There are two photos of Jason snuggled in blankets. He looks cute. And there's a photo of Mom and me, also from last year's barbecue. In the picture, Mom has her arm wrapped around me. I stare at the picture, knowing it's the last photo in which Mom will be looking proud of me. I sit at her desk and wait.

"Hey, Sarah." It's Anne Marie. "What's doing?"

"Nothing much." I swivel and look out the window, hoping Anne Marie will take the hint and leave.

"I just got back from the police station." She laughs. "I wasn't being arrested. I had to check *important* facts for a front-page story."

"That's nice."

"So what's it like working with Antonia DeMarco? It must be super cool."

"Oh, yes," I say. Wouldn't it make her day if I told her the truth? I'd rather stick needles in my eyes.

"Have you met any of her famous friends?"

"She invited me to a gathering," I say. "I met a couple of Hollywood producers. She's writing a screenplay."

"Wow," says Anne Marie. "You're making connections, girl." There is a look of total envy on her face. "Has she told you what the movie's about?"

I nod. "Actually, I helped her with the plot."

Anne Marie is staring with her mouth open. "Wow!" she gives me her phoniest smile. I'm enjoying her envy, and since it won't happen again, I decide to enhance it just a little.

"She's asked me to go off to Fiji with her," I lie.

"Fiji!"

"It's where she'll be writing the screenplay. I just don't know if I should go, you know. I'd miss my brother."

"Well . . . Fiji . . . huh," she sighs. "*Please* tell me what the movie is about."

I give her the cool look. "I'm not at liberty to say."

When Mom walks in, we both get up. "Mrs. Simmons," says Anne Marie, handing Mom the paper she was holding. "I spoke with Captain Jennings personally and double-checked all the facts."

"Thank you, Anne Marie." Mom tosses the paper on her desk and looks at me. Anne Marie smiles and walks out backward.

"Not that I'm not glad to see you," says Mom, "but can you explain why you are here, since you are grounded?"

I walk over to the door and close it. "Mom. You were right. Something is very wrong. We need to talk."

I stare at the floor as I tell her the truth. Mom gets really quiet at the part about the dent and how much I owe

Rent-a-Dream if I ever want to see the plays again. At this point, I look up and wish I hadn't. The skin on her face is tight, except for her forehead, which now has a million stress wrinkles on it. She's going to blow any second.

I wish she would yell and get it over with. Instead, she grabs her cell phone and dials. "Bert, it's Helen. I have a question. Do I have any grounds to take legal action against someone who has verbally agreed to judge a contest and then absconded with all the entries? No, she didn't sign anything." She continues her conversation with the *Courier*'s lawyer. I wait for the blast.

She gets off the phone but doesn't look at me. The silence is worse than yelling.

"Look, Mom, I take full responsibility for this. You tried to tell me that Antonia is irresponsible, but I wouldn't listen. If you loan me fifteen hundred dollars, I will straighten everything out. And I will get a job and pay back every penny."

She finally looks at me. "How long have you known that the plays were missing?"

"Since the night before last."

"You should have told me immediately."

"I know. I'm an idiot."

"First of all, you're not an idiot. I don't ever want you to say that again."

I nod, surprised by this.

"Now, while we're at it, let's find out the whole truth. Were you and Brendan with Antonia DeMarco that night?"

"Yes."

"Why did you go when I told you not to?"

"Because she needed my help with a personal problem."

"It's nice that you wanted to help her, but that doesn't make what you did right."

"I know. I've done a lot of things wrong lately, but I've learned from my mistakes."

She caresses my cheek. "That's good."

"I guess I'm not a daughter you can be proud of."

"Of course, I'm proud of you."

I shake my head. "You should have a daughter who's more like yourself. Someone logical. Someone who doesn't ruin contests."

She picks up my chin. "Stop. I've been doing a lot of thinking lately. I've watched you idolizing that woman. The worst part is, I was jealous. I've worked so hard to get where I am, and all along, in the back of my head, I had the hope that my daughter would someday find me amazing." She leans back and wrinkles her nose. "I guess it isn't easy being my daughter."

"It's not," I say.

She nods. "I work too hard protecting you from making the kinds of mistakes I made."

"You made a mistake?"

"Lots," she says. "When I was in college, I had a summer job in Ammazoli's campaign office. He made stirring speeches about saving Staten Island's parklands. I believed every word. The first thing he did after being elected was sell Adams Park to developers. Later, when I became a reporter, I found out that just before the sale, a large amount of money passed into his personal account. I felt ridiculous for believing in him, and I was angry. I spent so much time trying to link the money in his account to the sale of the park that I ignored a lot of my other work. I came dangerously close to losing my job. But I never found any evidence. I'm still angry that he got away with it. And now they've named a ferry boat after him."

"Still," I say. "You do all these great things like helping restore South Beach."

"Exactly," she says. "So people like Antonia can enjoy it." She laughs.

"I'm never going to do great things."

"You will. Be patient. You'll learn, unfortunately, by making mistakes like this one. Ammazoli made me realize I need to see facts before I make a commitment. That's what made me a good reporter, and a good editor." She puts my hand in hers. "I'll try to give you some space to have your own good learning experiences, but just a few, okay?"

I laugh. "Mom, I'm going to be a writer. Do you mind not coming up with any more great ideas for young writers, unless I can be a part of them, too?"

She bites her lip. "I'll keep that in mind." She walks back to her desk and sits. "So, you don't think Antonia DeMarco is amazing?"

"No."

"I'm so relieved," she mutters. "*Enraptured Thorns in My Heart.* What on earth does that mean?"

"I don't know." We both laugh. "Can you keep a secret?"

She nods.

"Antonia didn't write that book."

Mom's eyebrows shoot up. "She's a fake, too."

"Totally. Will you loan me the money?"

"No need," she says. "I made copies."

"You really didn't trust her?"

"Not one iota."

"Who will judge the contest?"

"I'll figure something out. Let me get back to work and we'll talk tonight."

I walk home in a daze. What do I do about my play? Would it be a mistake to hand it in, pretending to be Victoria? Or would this be one of those good learning experiences?

TWENTY-TWO

Hi Lynn,
Nothing's normal. I hate Antonia. I like my mother. Georgina is the inspiration for a movie. Jane Austen is better than Antonia. Brendan is sexy.
Abnormally yours, SOS

Hi Lynn,
Enraptured Thorns in My Heart is now a window jam.
SOS

Hi Lynn,
Oops—it fell into the mulch pile.
Stinkingly, SOS

Hi Lynn,
Mom is judge. What should I do with my play?
Need to know, SOS

Hi Lynn,
Let fate choose! Huh?
Baffled, confused, perplexed, SOS

Hi Lynn,
OK. Left play on hallway table near front door.
Fate-fully, SOS

Hi Lynn,
Play no longer on hallway table.
Nervously, SOS
P.S. Where is Brendan? With :)

Hi Lynn,
Thanks for postcard. U R the best!
5 days, 13 hours, 27 minutes = 0 Brendan!
Lonely, SOS

Dear Lynn,
New story. Girl named Sally meets idol, Angela.
Angela turns out to be jerk.
Mom found fiction contest in Teen magazine!
SOS
P.S. 7 days, 4 hours, 14 minutes = 0 Brendan!

It's around 5:00 and Mom's in the kitchen reading play number eleven of twenty-three. I bring her a glass of lemonade and some of the gingerbread cookies I baked for the fair tomorrow. They came out really good and the entire house smells of cinnamon and nutmeg. I never realized how relaxing baking cookies can be. I think I will become a writer who bakes.

"I just spoke with Dad," I say. "He's going to take us all to Germany next summer."

"Great," says Mom. By this time next year, I will be on my way to becoming a world traveler. Which is a very good thing for a writer to be.

Mom bites into a cookie. "Mmmm, delicious," she says. "How's Jason doing?"

"Not too cranky. Georgina's reading him a story."

"I'm glad she agreed to stay tonight so I can finish reading all the plays."

"Can I do anything to help?"

"I'll let you know." Things have been different between my mother and me in the last week. It's like we're on our best behavior. She surprised me with tickets to a Broadway show. Just the two of us, and we're going in two weeks—for fun. I surprised her, too, by signing up for music lessons. I got tired of looking at my dulcimer. I want to learn to make beautiful sounds.

"Don't worry about the programs for the fair," I say. "I'll help Beth."

She hasn't read my play yet, and I seriously think about snatching it when she's not looking. But I have to admit that I'm curious. Would Mom pick me if she didn't know it was me? In the future, I will work harder on being a stronger, more honest person.

The doorbell rings. It's Beth and Brendan with a

box of inserts for the programs. Brendan looks great in a plain denim shirt and khaki pants.

"Hi," I say.

Beth breezes in, talking about three things at once. Brendan says, "Hello." Where has he been for the last week? I lead them into the dining room. We're using the table to fold the programs for the fair. Beth shows me the insert, a small slip of paper that reads, "Antonia DeMarco apologizes for not being able to judge the teen writing contest, as she was called away on important business. She wishes all the contestants luck and success with their writing." It doesn't seem fair that no one will know that she almost ruined this contest, but Mom wants to keep it simple.

"It's a shame that Antonia had to leave so suddenly," says Beth. She rolls up her sleeves and begins taking programs out of the boxes and arranging them in page order. "I hope we'll still have a high attendance."

The three of us stand at the table collating the pages. There are three pages, plus the insert, which have to be collated and folded into a booklet. The program lists all the fair's events, like the pie-eating contest, the sack races, the singing contest, the writing contest, the list of vendors, and an invitation to the Preservation Ball, which takes place tomorrow night in the open-air pavilion.

Brendan grabs pages without really looking at what

he's doing. "Slow down," says Beth. "Page two usually precedes page three." She walks into the kitchen to talk to Mom.

"Hey," says Brendan. "A man rushes into the doctor's office and shouts, 'Doctor, I think I'm shrinking!' The doctor says, 'Now settle down. You'll just have to be a little patient.'"

I laugh.

"Do you think a paying audience will find that funny?"

How could I say no? "Well . . . sure."

He moves closer and whispers. "I'm on tonight at the Java Café at nine. I'm so nervous, but I've been practicing all week."

"Where?"

"Anywhere I could find an audience. Remember the nurses we met that day at the diner? I took their advice and told jokes in the emergency room. The guard asked me to leave after two hours, but he said I was funny. Then I rode all over the island. I found audiences at the mall, the post office, grocery stores, and in the ferry terminal. That was the best testing ground, since the boat is late a lot."

"That's great."

"Lots of people laughed at my jokes, but there were a lot who didn't. What if I get the non-laughers tonight? I'll bomb before I even start."

"You won't bomb." But I'm nervous for him. His jokes are kind of old. I'm glad to know where he's been all week. "Does your mom know about this evening?"

"Are you kidding? That's why I need your help. She's got a million things for me to do and I have to be out of here by 8:30. Let's hurry and finish."

I try to hurry, but when I do, the pages stick together. "Look," I say, grabbing the programs out of his hands. "I can take care of this by myself. I have all night. Why don't you go and get ready."

"Then how are you going to watch me perform?"

"You want me to come?"

"Yeah." He smiles. "I thought I'd pay you to laugh. You'd be a plant."

"What kind of plant?" I say, kidding.

"A laughing one."

I reach past him for a set of pages. "I can't. I'm still grounded."

"What does that have to do with anything?"

"Mom and I are trying to work things out, so I don't want to make her mad right now." Besides, there is something more important that I've been dying to find out.

"Uh, Brendan. I hope you got to meet whoever you were supposed to meet last week."

"Huh?"

"When we were at the diner, you told me you had to

go meet someone. It sounded like a very important meeting."

"Oh, yeah, I did. It was."

We continue to collate. Why can't he just tell me if it was Anne Marie?

"So, who was it?"

"Who?"

"The woman you were meeting."

He looks at me sideways and I'm embarrassed.

"Judith Meyers. She's the manager of the Java Café. She thinks I'm funny."

"That's great," I say too loud because I'm so excited it wasn't Anne Marie. I hope he thinks I'm happy that Judith thinks he's funny. Then I start wondering how old Judith is and if she likes Brendan.

Beth comes back into the dining room. "Can you two take care of the programs? I want to help your mother type her critiques."

"No problem," I say.

I move the folded programs into an empty box. "Have you invited anyone else?"

"No, just you."

I try not to show him how happy I am about that, too. To think I've been agonizing all week over Anne Marie being his girlfriend.

"Hey," I say. "What did Cinderella say when she left the photo store?" He shrugs. "Someday my prints will come."

He smiles. "Now, that is funny."

"Really?"

He leans in and kisses me. Wow! It took me three days to find one joke, but now I'm so glad I did.

Beth orders two pizzas and we take a break. Mom continues reading. I try not to stare at Brendan too much, especially his lips. Maybe next time, *I'll* kiss *him.* Thinking about this makes my face flush. I slip away to the kitchen to get lemonade. *Mom's reading my play.* I pivot on the spot and bolt back to the dining room.

Beth and Georgina talk about setting up the booths in the morning. I'm thinking about Mom's red pen, which is probably circling every missing comma, every exclamation point. She hates exclamation points.

"The banner on Forest Avenue looks lovely," says Georgina.

"It's a new one. Last year's was looking ratty."

What does Mom think of my play? I bet she hates it.

After we finish eating, Georgina helps us collate the programs and we finish by 7:30. Brendan waves goodbye to me. "Good luck," I mouth so no one else will hear.

Before he leaves, he whispers, "See you later."

TWENTY-THREE

I iron the Suzanne dress, which I'll be wearing at the fair.

"Hey," says Georgina, popping into my room. "I'm wearing this. What do you think?" She holds up one of my mother's Victorian dresses. It's a deep shade of blue with a lacy white bodice. I know she will look beautiful in it. Georgina volunteered to help me at the refreshment booth and to teach me how to waltz for the evening dance. I'm really starting to like her a lot. "I'd better go home and get some beauty rest."

"Um . . . Is Mom finished reading?"

She nods. "She said it was hard, but she made a decision."

"Oh, that's nice." I try to sound like I don't care.

"You're a winner with me," she says. "Tootles."

"Tootles." Does that mean I didn't win? Would Mom have told her? I look around for something to keep my mind off the contest. I sit and stare at Manhattan. It doesn't have the same aura it usually has. I pick up a book and begin reading and put it right down. I might as well get this over with.

I go downstairs, pretending I'm thirsty. Mom's in the kitchen, talking on her cell phone. The plays are in two neat piles on the table in front of her. I slowly pour myself some lemonade. Mom talks about tomorrow's schedule. Not to look like I'm hanging around, waiting to find out the winner, I open the freezer and take a long look. I shuffle things around. Mom asks Beth to oversee the vendors to make sure they've all paid to exhibit. I shuffle things around again. They talk some more. The freezer is making me cold, so I shut it and open the refrigerator door and shuffle things in there. I grab a carrot stick and nibble on it while I inspect Mom's houseplant. It looks dry, so I water it. I wash a glass that's sitting in the sink. Finally, Mom hangs up.

She stands up and stretches while I dry the glass. "Want some lemonade?"

"Sure."

I pour her a glass and she takes it. "So," I say. "It looks like you're done."

She rolls the glass along her forehead and closes her eyes. "Finally."

"Did you pick a winner?"

"I did, but it was hard."

"Oh, really." I sit across from her. "Tell me about it?"

"There's a lot of good writing in here." She points

to the plays. "I had it narrowed down to four for quite a while."

Which four?

"I thought I'd make a few copies of the first-place manuscript and ask people to play the various parts, instead of reading the entire thing myself." She sips some lemonade. "Want to play a part?"

Only if it's my play. "Maybe," I say.

"The winner is a well-researched play," she continues. "The dialogue could use some work." She yawns. "I think Anne Marie has potential for being a fine reporter."

My hand starts shaking and I have to put down my glass. "Anne Marie won?"

"Yes, but as I said before, it was a hard choice. Linda Gonzales wrote a little gem about an oyster fisherman that was very funny, but it wasn't as historically accurate as Anne Marie's."

I nod and get up. "I have to do something upstairs." I walk toward the door, not wanting to cry until I'm alone.

"Oh, sure. By the way, do you know who Victoria Winters Johnson is?"

I stop at the door, but don't turn around. "Why do you ask?"

"Well, I know all the contestants except for Victoria."

"She's probably new."

"Probably," says Mom. "If she comes to the fair, I'd like to talk to her. I was quite moved by her play. It hit a chord with me."

I turn around. "Really?"

"Yes. It's about Suzanne Anderson. The girl who lived in this house. She carved her initial in our bathroom."

"Oh, the *S*," I say, pointing upstairs.

"That's the one," says my mother. "The play is good and very well written, but the dialogue is too modern and, most important, many of the facts aren't accurate. Victoria has Suzanne marrying Richard, but in reality she never got to marry him, because he died in the Battle of Fredericksburg."

"He did?"

"He did."

"Oh." Poor Suzanne!

"I wrote all the inaccuracies down in my critique. I also wrote that I think Victoria is a promising writer, but that a contest whose focus is on historical content is probably not the right contest for her. I suggested that she look into fiction contests because she has quite a talent for writing to the emotional heart of a situation."

I don't speak because there's something warm rising in my throat. Somehow I make my way out of the kitchen and up to my room.

It's weird, but I'm really not upset. I think there is a slight possibility that Mom has figured out that I'm

Victoria, but she's not saying, and I don't think she ever will. I'll enter the *Teen* magazine contest and use it to express the emotional heart of my feelings for Antonia.

It's weird, but even though I thoroughly despise Antonia, I'm glad I got to know her. If we hadn't met, I'd still be idolizing someone who didn't exist. If I'm going to be a writer, then I have to be more flexible about people. And I don't have to spend so much time looking for mysterious strangers, when the people I know have lots of mysterious things going on inside them. They can be just as interesting as royalty or movie stars. I'll write about Antonia and all the ways that she has messed up her life. And Georgina and Brendan—I'll write about how they have to practice their dreams in secret. And Mom and me—I'll write about people who made a mistake because they believed in the wrong person.

I open my bedroom window and stick my head out and gaze at the full moon. Brendan needs me. What if no one else laughs? I grab a notepad and a pen.

Mom,

I'm at the Java Café and will be home by 10. Sorry, but I have to go. A friend needs my support. I will be very careful.

Love you, Sarah

I prop the pad against my bed pillow and walk back to the window. I have fifteen minutes to get there. I'm planning to make it in seven.